THE BRITISH EMPIRE OF MAGIC

AND

THE DARK KNIGHTS' KING

JOSEPH J. JORDAN

© JOSEPH J. JORDAN

PROLOGUE

This, the second instalment of the British Empire of Magic trilogy, finds Jacob, now King of the British Empire of Magic and his imperial city still under siege from Thomas, King of the Dark Knights and his American allies. Jacob devises a plan to rescue his father from the White Islands and sends his partner, Co-Regent Lord Elliot, to Dover Cliff to retrieve the Members of Parliament before King Thomas can find them and take complete control of the Empire, but Jacob and Elliot grow suspicious that a traitor could be at the highest level within the Royal Council. Meanwhile, the last command of Queen Ellaryne to send Royal Lady Camilla Kerr to the French Kingdom of Magic to plead with King Jean for aid is failing. Camilla is lost within the maddening Finders Maze.

Suspicions grow and betrayal looms as truths are revealed and enemies become friends and allies become foes. The fight for the throne and future of all MagiFolk hangs in the balance as Jacob must stop Thomas from his ultimate goal… to wage a final war upon the human world.

CHAPTER 1

THE FINDERS MAZE AND KING JEAN OF THE FRENCH KINGDOM OF MAGIC

Hours had passed since Royal Lady Kerr and the Passing Dome's caretaker had been sent through the archway that was meant to lead to King Jean's villa but instead, they found themselves trapped within an endless maze with darkened thick glass-like walls towering imposingly above them. The ground they walked on was soft and squidgy with a grey mist floating up to their knees. Every turn they took was identical to the last and the maddening nature of it all was testing Lady Kerr's impatience.

"This is ridiculous! We don't have time for this. It's been hours and we are no closer from getting out of this infuriating maze," Lady Kerr said desperately.

The caretaker stopped and raised her eyebrows in surprise causing Lady Kerr to turn around and face her.

"What is it?" asked Lady Kerr, impatiently.

"*That's the first words you've spoken since we first arrived here,*" said the old lady caretaker, her voice soft and fragile.

Lady Kerr sighed and nodded. "*I'm sorry. It's just that I thought we would have found the French King by now and at least made a plan to help our people… we've been here hours and we can't even find our way back to the Passing Arch to get home or any way out for that matter!*"

The caretaker smiled knowingly, "*It's not that kind of maze my lady. We don't find a way out because there is none. It's a Finders Maze.*"

Lady Kerr frowned in confusion and anger, "*What in the Queen's name is a Finders Maze?*"

"*It's a maze designed to keep its visitors here until the owner wishes for them to be found,*" said the caretaker as she shrugged. "*It's really quite simple,*" she continued.

"*And you didn't think to share this with me when we arrived or maybe at some point in the last four hours?!*" said Lady Kerr, outraged.

"*I thought you knew. A lady of your standing and education…*" The caretaker smiled and continued to walk on.

Shaking her head and taking several deep breaths, Lady Kerr also continued their seemingly endless journey within the Finders Maze. "*Well… I didn't! So…? How exactly are we to be found?*"

"Whenever King Jean desires it, I would presume," replied the caretaker.

"Why would the Queen knowingly send me here if she knew I'd be trapped and just waiting?" Lady Kerr questioned aloud.

The caretaker looked at the Lady Kerr and shrugged.

"What is your name anyway? I can't just keep calling you The Caretaker," continued Lady Kerr.

"My name is Harriet Barthmide Trenston-Opal Juden," she said proudly but in a slightly humorous way.

Lady Kerr chuckled slightly, "Indeed. I'll call you Harriet if you don't mind. And as it seems it's just you and I in here for a while, you can call me Camila."

Harriet nodded and then, without any warning, a blinding flash of white light forced them both to fall to the ground and shield their faces. The walls of darkened glass and ground shook uncontrollably and as the blinding light began to subside, the world around them began to spin and shrink. They both reached out for each other's hand and held themselves close as their stomachs lurched as if they were falling from a great height. Suddenly everything stopped. Their eyes still closed tight, they could feel solid ground beneath their feet.

"Oh! I am sorry about that! Bonsoir, mesdames," said King Jean.

Camila and Harriet opened their eyes to a blurry vision as they tried to steady themselves. Camila the first to get to her feet. She helped Harriet up from the ground.

"*What is going on?*" Camila demanded while still dazed and confused with her surroundings, still holding Harriet's hand.

"*Yes, yes, I am sorry. The exit from the maze is always awful the first time, especially when you're not expecting it!*" King Jean's voice was smooth and his French accent so soft it was almost undetectable while he spoke in perfect English. The King was a very tall, thin old man; in fact, his age was a mystery to everyone and he never disclosed it. His eyes were a faded brown, his face long and drawn with his cheek bones protruding more than normal. He was dressed in a dark red flowing silk night robe and matching slippers, with a crown embroidered in gold.

Camila was now starting to get her bearings about where she was. Grey and white bricks lined the walls of a huge living room space within what she had now guessed was the King's villa. A roaring fire encased in a square cage of iron bars lay floating in the middle of the room, throwing flickering shadows across the room's curved arches leading outside. The long red curtains were blowing gently from the warm southern French night air. It was a peaceful and safe place.

"*Welcome to my villa, Lady Kerr,*" continued the King, "*and you must be...?*" The King looked down at Harriet.

"Harriet, Your Majesty. I am the Passing Dome Caretaker." The King looked slightly surprised for a second.

"The Caretaker you say? Surprising that your people have left the Dome without it's captain, so-to-speak," queried the King.

"My son Lennard is more than capable in my absence," replied Harriet proudly and matter-of-factly.

"I see. Interesting," said King Jean who nodded slowly as he looked the both of them up and down. Even through his vastly wrinkled thin face and grey stubble, they sensed he was a little displeased with their appearance.

"I assume your attire is a result of the fact that your country is on fire? I mean that both figuratively and literally of course," said King Jean

"Then you are aware of the situation, Your Majesty?" replied Camila.

The King nodded and raised his arm to motion them towards a large dark red chaise longue by the floating iron-caged fire. Camila and Harriet walked over and sat down while the King sat on an old creaky wooden chair opposite. It was at that moment the both of them realised just how tired they were from the hours of wandering through the maze.

"I assume both of you would care for a cognac," asked the King as he flicked his wrist towards a drinks' cabinet at the far end of the room. The cabinet doors opened and a decanter full of cognac and three crystal tumblers floated through the air towards them while the decanter poured the cognac into the tumblers. Camila and Harriet took the tumblers and sipped the cognac thankfully.

"*Yes, the news reached me early this afternoon. It is why I kept you in the Finders Maze for so long. Amongst the maze's many abilities, it masks anyone one who enters it from the outside world. Only the owner of the maze can reach them. So, you see, it was for your safety. I knew if you were coming here, it was under your Queen's command and it was best to keep you in there for the time being.*" The King motioned towards a large glass ornament from where they had just walked. Camila tilted her head while she looked at it and her head snapped back, her eyebrows raised high in surprise.

"*Is that, that is the Finders Maze?*" asked Camila.

The King chuckled lightly. "*They are incredible creations, no? Something so small yet so powerful.*"

Camila was amazed for a moment but quickly the reality of why she was there returned to her mind as she looked back at the King squarely in his eyes.

"*Your Majesty, I have indeed been sent here with urgent news from my Queen. A true blood descendent of King Colet of the Dark Knights has led an army of MagiWolfs and their masters to the gates of the Imperial City. He follows the same beliefs of his ancestors and plans to wage a war of all wars against the human world after defeating us. This King Thomas has also* allied with the American Republic of Magic and has the full use of their navy which is currently surrounding the city and the Royal Palace. I was sent here by my Queen to ask for your help and to ask you to come to our aid. Prince Jacob, the Queen's son, is leading our Imperial Guard in an effort to protect the Royal Palace and save whoever is left alive in the city but there is no telling how long they can hold off King Thomas's forces or even if he has. My Queen told me you would know what this means for us all."

   The King sat perfectly still for a moment staring out into the night though the stone arches and then took a single sip of his cognac before turning his gaze to Camila.

   "Your Queen and I have been close for many years and before that her father and I shared many truths… one of those truths was the tragedy of the Colsom family and who the father and son were descended from, the Colets… the very last of the line. I told him then that you cannot stop an evil force by committing an equally evil act. MagiNature has a way of balancing itself out. Thomas is the weight that balances the scales of MagiNature. Yes, Lady Kerr, the French Kingdom of Magic will come to your aid and defeat this King Thomas and his allies." Camila closed her eyes briefly and sighed in relief at the King's agreement to help. The King began to stand up slowly from his chair, grunting as he did so.

   "No doubt this King Thomas has convinced the Lady Regent Catherine of the White Islands to open the barrier allowing the American Republic of Magic and their navy to cross… That was a rhetorical question, Lady Kerr… We must travel to Palais de

Vol immediately to raise my army and navy," announced King Jean. Camila and Harriet stood up at once.

"Palais de Vol? My French isn't what it used to be but… A flying palace, Your Majesty?" queried Camila.

The King looked amused and shuffled over closer to her and Harriet as he shrugged with both his palms raised up level with his shoulders, "Ahhh, it's more floating than flying but yes, that is close enough," he chuckled and motioned them out towards one of the archways leading outside. "Come. This way. We must leave at once," he continued.

The three made their way through the grey and white brick archway and out onto a stone patio overlooking an ocean glistening in the moonlight. Below them Camila could see the lit roads and fast-moving lights across them. She had seen these things before, creations from the human world… Cars.

"Is this a passing arch?" asked Harriet as she looked back at the archway touching the stone wall.

"No, no, nothing as traceable as that. We will go the French way." The King pointed out over the ocean at an object approaching them at high speed.

The closer the object came, the more Camila and Harriet could make out the shape of a perfect golden sphere. As it reached the patio where they were stood, they could see the surface of the thirty-foot golden sphere was rippling as if it was water. Camila and Harriet marvelled at it even though neither of them knew what it was.

The King began to laugh softly as he looked at Camila's reaction to the sphere.

"Your Queen Ella told me about you, Lady Camila Kerr. She spoke highly. She also told me you've been to many places in this world but never to the French Kingdom. Why is that? My Kingdom holds many wonders."

Camila met the King's gaze plainly, "perhaps that's a story for another time, Your Majesty, and if I may ask… if your Kingdom is so wondrous, why have you chosen to live here in the human world?" said Camila.

"Anonymity and privacy are precious commodities at my age and position… and I wish to hear that story one day but time is not on our side right now, is it?… Come," said King Jean as he rested his hand on the surface on the sphere causing the ripples to hasten. Quickly a hole had started to appear with the ripples pulling back the edges, making it wider and wider. Soon enough the hole was big enough for the three of them to step inside. With King Jean leading the way, they entered the sphere, sealing itself behind them.

Camila and Harriet were amazed by what they now saw. There were ten white heavily cushioned seats in a perfect circle facing a floating silver globe spinning slowly in the middle. The walls surrounding them were golden and rippling in the same way as the exterior. The King held out his hand, motioning towards the seats as he slowly shuffled his way to sit down. *"Please, both of you, take a seat and we can be on our way."*

Camila and Harriet made their way to the white cushioned seats facing the spinning globe and sat down. Camila looked at King Jean who was reaching out touching the spinning globe, tapping it in the middle of what looked like somewhere in the middle of the Mediterranean Sea. The globe instantly zoomed in closer and this time, it showed a jagged object that looked like an island to Camila's eye with a palace atop. The King tapped it again and then suddenly they were forced backward into their seats with the g-force of the sphere moving. The three of them were on their way to Palais de Vol - The Flying Palace.

CHAPTER TWO

KING JACOB

Night had now fallen over the Royal Palace and Imperial City. The American Republic of Magic's navy still surrounded the island and the flames from their bombardment still roared throughout the city streets. Thankfully the Imperial Guard had evacuated most of the city's residents behind the barrier which was now protecting the Royal Palace.

Atop the Higher Palace in the Queen's apartment, Jacob sat silently and still at the end of his mother's bed watching her, still in his plain and fire-singed robes.

The familiar sand stone walls and floating fire spheres lit the room. Long white draping banners adorning the royal crest floated in mid-air either side of the Queen's bed.

The doctor's attempts to wake her had been unsuccessful since she fell from Thomas's attack above the palace. She was alive and that was enough good news to keep Jacob moving forward for now. He reached out and took her hand in his and closed his eyes. He focused his mind and allowed his magic to flow through his body and reach out to her mind but all he could see was an emptiness within her, no thoughts or feelings. Perhaps distantly he could sense her but she was somewhere else. He opened his eyes and broke the connection. He sighed heavily and cast his deep brown eyes up to the ceiling.

"I know you're there, mother. Somewhere. I will find you and bring you back. I just hope I can give you an Empire to come back too."

"We will! Because KING Jacob has a plan!" said Elliot

"When did you sneak in?" replied Jacob. Elliot stood to the left side of the apartment doorway. Dressed in a simple long blue robe, his blonde hair was still dirtied from the rubble of the city and his bright blue eyes were fixed on Jacob.

"Oh, I've been here for a little while. I didn't want to interrupt the conversation you were having with yourself!" Elliot said with sarcastic smile.

Jacob stood up from the Queen's bed and walked over to Elliot. "Are you actually trying to be funny in a time like this?" snapped Jacob.

"Crikey! If we lose our humour, what's the point?" Elliot replied as he smiled at Jacob.

Jacob smiled back warmly. "So childish! I knew having a younger partner would come back to haunt me one day!" They both laughed and hugged each other firmly. Elliot took Jacob's hands in his and stared into his eyes.

"How are you?" asked Elliot.

"Holding up. I've tried reaching out to her mind but there's something stopping me or she's just not there... I can't explain it. Is there still no word from Camila?" Jacob said desperately.

"No, no word yet... but she's been there for less than a day. We have to give her more time," said Elliot as he looked over Jacob's shoulder at the Queen. "She will come through this, Jacob. No one living has seen spells as powerful as that and lived. She is alive and she gave as good as she got, so I think she can handle this... whatever it is she's going through," continued Elliot.

Jacob turned around and walked over to the window overlooking the burning city below with Elliot following close behind him.

"Time is something I don't think we have but you're right, we have to trust Camila will be successful in convincing the French King to come to our aid. In the meantime, there are things we can do here. I want you to go to Parliament House at Dover Cliff and find out what the situation is with the Paramilitary Members there. Hand pick a small group of the best Imperial guards that you trust and take them with you. I have no doubt Thomas will be searching for the entrance already. If he finds them before we get to them…" Jacob turned to face Elliot staring straight into his eyes, *"Parliament represent the people and if Thomas coerces Parliament to his bidding, we lose the people. We lose it all,"* said Jacob while Elliot nodded confidently in agreement.

"And then what? What will you do?" asked Elliot.

"My father is still captured on the White Islands and I have to get him back. We have Neville. While Thomas would never agree to it, he isn't on the White Islands and I think Kendra could be persuaded to do a prisoner trade. My father for her husband."

"What makes you think you can convince Kendra to do that? I know she loves him but—?" asked Elliot.

*"Kendra and Neville recently had a child – a boy, only a few months old by my understanding. Kendra knows what it's like

to grow up without a father and won't want that for her son. She'll agree," said Jacob.

"Even if you could convince Kendra, there is no way her mother, The Lady Regent, would go for it! You'd still have to break your father out!"

"Oh, if I know my father, he is already working on a way out and if Kendra is onboard with the swap… I just have to be near when the moment comes."

"You're not seriously thinking of going there alone?" Elliot said outraged.

"Apart from the Imperial Guards holding Neville, I will be alone; I have to be. Anything else will draw too much attention," replied Jacob as Elliot shook his head and started pointing his finger at Jacob.

"There is no way I am letting you do this without me!" demanded Elliot.

Jacob took Elliot's pointing hand, lowering it and smiled. "You can't. If I am captured you must take the throne; you are co-regent and with that comes a responsibility. It's dangerous enough for us to be doing two separate errands let alone doing one together. Thomas cannot be in two places at once so he will have to choose one of us to attack IF he finds us… You know I speak sense," said Jacob as he placed his hand on Elliot's shoulder. Elliot looked down at the sand-coloured stone ground, in submission, and sighed.

"I do. I also know if he has to choose which one of us he'll come for; it'll be you and that's what scares me," replied Elliot.

Jacob turned back around to look out over the burning city. "Hiding from him will only delay the inevitable. This only ends when he and I face each other again." Jacob's voice was unwavering and strong.

"With both of us gone what about here? The palace and our people?" asked Elliot as he looked below to the lower palace courtyard.

"There will be enough of the guard to protect it and the Royal Councillors will stay here. Most of them are powerful enough even if a lifetime of politics has made them forget that... talking of which, Lady Black will be here shortly. I am placing her in command of the palace and city while we are away." Elliot looked at Jacob and frowned in surprise.

"Lady Black? She's not your biggest fan, is she? Especially after you named me co-regent. Why her?" Elliot asked.

Jacob chuckled lightly and smiled, "That's precisely why I am placing her in charge. Nothing brings a person round into your favour better than patting their ego."

Elliot laughed and shook his head at Jacob. "That's clever."

Jacob turned around and walked back towards his mother's bedside, looking down at her. "I've learnt a few things from her over the years," Jacob said proudly.

Suddenly a soft knocking came at the apartment door.

"*Yes?*" answered Jacob.

The door swung open and the slight figure of Royal Lady Black entered the room, her short dark hair shining in the fire light. She was dressed in a fitted white military-style jacket and dark fitted trousers with a bright silver belt around her waist, encrusted with the royal crest. Her eyes were the darkest of brown and were fixed on Jacob.

"*Your Highness? You sent for me?*" Lady Black's voice was monotoned and mid-pitched. Elliot immediately interjected, stepping in between Jacob and Lady Black

"*Forgive me, Lady Black, but I believe it's 'Your Majesty' now?*"

Lady Black snapped her head to look at Elliot. He could tell she was desperately trying to hide any expression on her face while Jacob looked down at the ground, smiling subtly.

"*Quite right, Lord Elliot. My apologies, Your Majesty,*" Lady Black said quietly.

"*I've only been King for half a day Lady Black. I'm still getting used to it myself,*" replied Jacob comically as he walked over to meet her. "*You found the son of the Passing Dome's Caretaker? Is he able to operate the arches?*" Jacob continued.

Lady Black nodded sharply. "*Yes, luckily he was one of the people the Imperial Guards evacuated into the palace during the* attack. His mother has been teaching him to take her place and is confident he can open the archways to Colghorn as well as the White Islands and Dover Cliff. Are you sure this is wise, Your Majesty? The both of you leaving the palace?"

"Yes, Lady Black I am. Besides, you are here with the rest of the Royal Council to look after things in our absence," replied Jacob.

"Forgive me Your Majesty but you are leaving us with no blood relative for succession. If the worst should happen to either of you and no heir?" Lady Black said sternly while also glancing at Elliot who was narrowing his eyes at her.

"Indeed, Lady Black. Desperate times unfortunately. Have the Caretaker's son meet us at the Passing Dome first thing in the morning," Jacob replied, with a regal command in his voice.

Lady Black turned on her heel to leave. "And keep an eye out for Camila while I'm gone. There is no telling how she will return but if it is with the French fleet, make sure they stay hidden from Thomas's forces. The element of surprise must be ours," Jacob continued as Lady Black glanced back and nodded in acknowledgement.

Elliot waved the back of his hand across the space in front of him, summoning a pushing spell to close the door behind Lady Black. The door slammed with a loud bang and Elliot turned to face Jacob with rage in his eyes, his fists clenched.

"What in the Queen's name did she mean by that?!" Elliot bellowed.

"Elliot, calm down. She's frightened. We all are. For the first time in most of our lives, our future is threatened. Our position on top of this magical world has fallen," Jacob said calmly as Elliot pointed back at the apartment door.

"And that gives her the right to criticise or remark about you not having an heir?" Elliot's anger was building more intensely as he spoke.

Jacob breathed in deeply and walked over to Elliot, holding his arms and looking into his eyes. "It does, because I'm King of her country or at least until my mother wakes up and you're my partner in life and love. Some of them don't understand that or what it means for them or us in the future. We broke the rules a long time ago, Elliot. I'm proud of that and I know you are too. After all this is over, the family that you and I create together, that will be the future of this Empire. I want to spend the rest of my life with you and I think it's time we made it official," Jacob said while smiling widely, looking into Elliot's blue eyes which were now glassing over with emotion.

"Are you… asking me to mar—?" Jacob cut Elliot off by placing his index finger on Elliot's ring finger. A subtle gold light sparked between his and Elliot's fingers as Jacob moved his finger around the sides of Elliot's. A thin gold band began to appear around Elliot's finger until the edges joined each other. Elliot's mouth was wide open in surprise and shock; he looked down at his hand where now a perfect golden ring was wrapped around his finger.

"That's a wedding ring, Jacob!" Elliot said, his voice shaking and body trembling.

"Ah, there's no fooling you is there!? So, are you going to keep it on?" asked Jacob as he took a step back.

Tears now running down Elliot's face, they both smiled at each other and started laughing.

"I'm never taking it off!" cried Elliot as he looked up from the ring and towards the Queen. Jacob followed his gaze while smiling and nodding.

"If you're wondering what she would think, she'd approve alright. In fact, I think she'd ask why it's taken so long!" Jacob laughed, *"it's right that we are doing this here, with her. She'd hate to miss out."*

Jacob's eyes began to fill as Elliot pulled his arm back round to him and the two embraced each other. For a moment the happiness between them dissolved the worry and tragedy surrounding them and their Empire.

CHAPTER THREE

A MOTHER'S LOVE

Deep beneath the old manor, Regent's Hall, through a series of darkly lit stairwells, are the dungeons of the White Islands. The darkness, cold and despair was in every corner of the long cavern. The faint but relentless dripping of water leaked through from the foul weather that was battering the main island of Farland above. So cold and damp were the dungeons that even the guards couldn't last a day on duty without getting soaked and cold. Three of these guards lined a long corridor of the cavern of wet black stone. Only one fire torch was lit along the stone wall. The dungeon cells opposite the wall were all empty except for the very last one where the third guard stood watch. The tall and broad-shouldered figure of Prince Johnathan lay motionless on the floor of his cell. His robe was torn and soaking wet, his hands locked behind him with a binding spell rendering his magic useless. The guard, who was dressed in a black fur coat that wrapped around his neck and almost touched the bottom of the stone floor, peered into Johnathan's cell.

"*Oi! You awake in there?*" the guard quietly whispered. Even in the dim light you could see the condensation from his breath filling the cold air above him.

Johnathan began to move gently out of his foetal-like position with a few protesting grunts. Rolling onto his back, he lifted himself so he could sit crossed legged facing the guard. As Johnathan looked up, the dim fire light rested on his face revealing the cuts and bruises and a badly swollen left eye. He narrowed and focused his good eye at the guard and smiled.

"*So… you have news for me, Tom?*" Johnathan's deep-timbred voice echoed through the dungeon.

"*Shhh! There's other guards down here you know!*" Tom leant in a little closer towards the cell door. "*Our agreement? It stands?*" continued Tom.

Johnathan chuckled and nodded "*I told you… they can't keep me down here forever and when they move me, I'll request you stay on as my prisoner guard as a condition of my cooperation. You want to get out of this job, don't you?*" Tom nodded while he took a paranoid glance down the corridor towards the other guards. "*So, what can you tell me about the battle?*" Johnathan continued.

"*The Dark Knight King Thomas and his American lot have taken your Imperial City. He and The Queen, um… your wife, were fighting. Big fight as I hear it and—*" Johnathan cut off Tom mid-sentence and pushed his face hard up against the cell bars.

"Is she alright? Do you know what happened?" He couldn't hide the desperation in his voice.

Tom knelt down and whispered through the cell's bars. "Dunno. I was told Prince Jacob got in the middle of the fight. Took the Queen back to the Royal Palace and created some kind of barrier which is still stopping King Thomas from getting to her or the rest of your lot," said Tom as Johnathan rocked backwards from the cell bars and looked down at the ground smiling.

"I don't think it's what King Thomas had planned," continued Tom.

"I'd bet it wasn't!" laughed Johnathan. "How many of King Thomas's forces are here on Farland, Tom?"

Tom pursed his lips and looked around at the other guards again. "You know I can't tell you that," said Tom.

"And you know I can't help you unless you help me, Tom," replied Johnathan.

Tom sighed and looked back at Johnathan reluctantly. "You better do what you say you will… There's only one American battle ship ere'; the rest have been sent to the Imperial City," said Tom.

Johnathan shuffled his way across his cell floor to rest his back up against the damp, cold wall. "*Thank you, Tom, I—*"

Johnathan stopped talking at once as he could hear footsteps coming down the dark stairwell in front of his cell. Tom also heard them and stood up at once and took several paces back towards his guard station by the black stone wall.

Johnathan bent his head down low to look up towards the steep stairwell at the figure making their way down to the dungeon cells. As the figure came to the bottom of the stairs, Johnathan could now make out it was possibly a woman of average height dressed in a hooded dark grey fur robe. The hooded figure now stood directly in front of Johnathan's cell and looked down the corridor towards Tom and the other guards and lowered her hood. Her thick long blond hair glowed dimly in the fire light.

"*Leave us,*" said the woman. The guards all looked at each other, unsure what to do. "*No doubt you will all be eager for a break and to get some warmth top side? Go… and do not return until I have left,*" she continued.

Tom was the first to reply, "*As you wish Lady Kendra.*"

The guards all left the dungeons through the dark stairwell, leaving just Kendra and Johnathan alone. After she was sure that Tom and the rest of the guards had left, she turned her head and looked down at Johnathan. Her piercing blue eyes even shone brightly in the dungeon light. The two looked at each other for moment in silence until Johnathan twisted his body around and rested his left shoulder on the stone wall so he could face Kendra.

"*Come here to gloat, Kendra?*" Johnathan's face may have been badly bruised and cut but his glare was as clear and intimidating as she remembered it to be.

Kendra shook her head slowly. "*Not quite. I'm here because I know you are planning to escape.*"

Johnathan rolled his head back in surprise, "*And what makes you think that?*"

Kendra smiled, "*There isn't much that happens on this island that I don't know about. For instance, the little game of manipulation you're playing with the guard, Tom.*"

Johnathan narrowed his gaze at Kendra. "*What do you want?*" he said plainly.

"*Why do you think that I want something?*" asked Kendra as she tilted her head to one side.

"*Clearly you haven't told anyone about the guard, Tom. Instead, you've come to me first. If you didn't want anything from me, you would have told your mother and had Tom arrested.*"

Kendra stared down at Johnathan, hiding any expression from him.

"*So? What is it you want?*" continued Johnathan.

"*I've received word that your son is offering a prisoner exchange. You for Neville.*" Kendra's eyes narrowed. "*He sent word to me directly because he no doubt knows my mother wouldn't agree to the exchange but I can convince her," Kendra continued.

Johnathan shuffled away from the wall so he could square up to Kendra as best he could. *"That may be so, but that doesn't really answer my question. Why are you here telling me this?"* Johnathan said, genuinely confused.

Kendra lent down closer to him. *"During the exchange, I want you to guarantee my son and I can come with you and grant us asylum in the British Empire."*

Johnathan's confusion had now reached its peak but was overridden by intrigue as he frowned deeply. *"Why do you or your son need to leave this place the very moment when your husband, the father of your child has returned?"* asked Johnathan.

Kendra straightened her back and took a glance behind her to check they were still alone, *"because Neville is not my baby's father,"* Kendra said plainly, without any emotion, while Johnathan's mouth opened slightly, but he realised it was showing his surprise at what she said so he closed it quickly and coughed, hiding his disbelief.

"It is no longer safe for my son here. King Thomas's plan was to take the Royal Palace, the Imperial City along with the entire Royal Council, the Queen and your son in one fell swoop. But he failed. The Queen is said to be alive and your son is now King. No doubt he is also securing aid… most likely from the French Kingdom. This war was meant to be over as soon as it started. I

can't have my son be victim to his parents' actions. He must be on the right side of this." Kendra's voice was clear and decisive.

Johnathan was now staring at Kendra, studying her, his mind racing as he drew his conclusion about who the boy's father was.

"Your son? His father… it's Thomas Colet, isn't it? Does Thomas know? Does Neville?" said Johnathan as Kendra's shoulders moved in an irritated and impatient way.

"Astute as ever Johnathan. No, neither of them knows but soon they will. One way or another Thomas will sense it and I have seen him do things to people in his anger, things I didn't know were possible. My son can't be subject to that or his mother's poor decisions… Will you agree to what I have asked and will your son accept it?"

Johnathan retuned to lean his shoulder on the cold and wet stone wall while still looking at Kendra and nodding slowly. "I will agree, Kendra. So will my son. But we will have to be clever about this. Get your mother to agree to the exchange and to make sure King Thomas knows nothing of it. An opportunity to get to my son out in the open and alone will be too tempting for him to ignore. Whatever method Jacob uses to get here, you and your son will have to be close to it and hidden. If I can get this binding spell weakened by the time Jacob gets here, I may be able to communicate with him when we are close enough, using a mind spell."

"I will not be able to help you with the binding spell. It will be too obvious I'm involved," Kendra replied with a hint of concern in her voice.

"The binding spell your guards have me in, it's powerful because all three of the guards down here cast the spell together. However, as with all cooperative spells, if you break the link between the casters, the spell weakens."

Kendra looked back towards the stairwell and then returned to look at Johnathan. "*And you think you can convince Tom to be that break in the casting link?*" asked Kendra.

Johnathan shrugged. "*He's been useful enough so far. I don't think it's much more of a leap to think he will help an old man out with an over-powerful binding spell, to just weaken it slightly. Just for comfort, of course.*" Johnathan smiled slightly and for the first time, Kendra looked happy.

Kendra placed her hood back up and turned around to face the stairwell. "*Be ready Prince Johnathan. I'm trusting you with my son's life,*" and she climbed the stairwell out of Johnathan's view. He lowered his head and puffed out his cheeks. "*I wasn't expecting that,*" he whispered to himself.

CHAPTER FOUR

PALAIS DE VOL - THE FLYING PALACE

Over two hundred miles south of the human French city of Marseille and five thousand feet above the Mediterranean Sea is the island of the Flying Palace – the capital state of the French Kingdom of Magic which was protected and hidden from the humans by the same masking spells that surround the Imperial City.

The golden sphere transporting Royal Lady Kerr, Harriet the Passing Dome caretaker and King Jean was now climbing fast up along the half jagged, half tree-root-covered cliff edges of the flying island. Gigantic waterfalls with cascading water falling from the cliffs dropped to the air below, forming white spray and disappearing long before reaching the ocean thousands of feet below.

Inside the sphere, they were all still seated while King Jean raised his hand towards one of the golden rippling walls of the sphere where it began to change and go transparent revealing an uninterrupted view of their destination.

The King smiled at Camila and Harriet. His deeply wrinkled and thinning face couldn't hide his expression of pride.

"Welcome to Palais de Vol!" said King Jean as Camila and Harriet's expressions showed clear signs of awe. Camila could see the huge waterfalls along the edges of the island but as they climbed higher, this huge island began to reveal its beauty. Grey and white stoned buildings of various sizes, from a small house to enormous manors, scattered the island's edges. The island was over a hundred miles wide and now they began to fly towards what Camila guessed was the centre of the island. More buildings began to come into her focus but the closer they got to the centre of the islands, the more dense the buildings became, separated only by the tall trees with huge canopies between them. The city below was now a sea of green from the trees and grey and white of the buildings. The beauty of it was truly enough to render Camila and Harriet speechless.

"There!" said King Jean pointing to a huge needle-shaped building of white stone rising over three thousand feet in the air. So high was this pointed building that the top was obscured by the clouds it nestled in.

"That is the Central Palace. This is where we will raise my army and navy," continued King Jean.

The sphere began to climb quickly once again towards the very top of the Palace where, finally, they began to slow as they approached one side of the curved wall of the palace about a hundred feet from the top. Coming to a complete stop, the sphere hovered for a few moments in front of the smooth solid wall of the palace until the stones began to rattle and, one by one, began to rotate and slide out of place revealing an entrance just big enough for the sphere to fly through. Slowly they began to move through this newly created hole in the palace wall. The sphere set down on the surface now inside the palace as the hole began to close behind them.

"We are here. Come we must go; there is no time to waste," said King Jean as he awkwardly got up from his chair inside the sphere and clapped his hands together, motioning Camila and Harriet to do the same. As commanded, they got up from their chairs and followed the King towards the golden wall opposite them where another hole was appearing, identical to the first hole they entered through. The golden wall ripped backwards and they stepped out through the exit following the King into the darkness of the palace.

As they stepped down onto the ground of the palace, the darkness was instantly replaced by lines of fire racing along the floor in front of them and up the walls lighting the entire hangar which they were now in. A large bang came from the left of the hangar which made Harriet jump in surprise.

Camila looked to where the sound came from and a door had opened with a small group of five men dressed in white three-quarter length tight-fitted trousers and perfectly tailored white military studded tops. They approached them in a flawless synchronised walking march and stopped just a few paces in front of King Jean with the man at the front stomping his right foot as he stopped with a huge clap that echoed through the hangar and speaking in French to King Jean who nodded his head in response and shuffled over towards the white uniformed man, placing his hand on his shoulder, looking directly into his eyes and then looking past to the men standing behind silently.

"We have guests from the British Empire. Let's speak in their tongue, shall we?" said King Jean looking back at Camila and Harriet. *"These gentlemen are my privy council... gentleman, meet Royal Lady Kerr and... Harriet of the British Empire of Magic,"* continued King Jean in a slight comical tone. The privy council all nodded towards Camila and Harriet.

"Ready the fleet and my entire army. We must sail to the Imperial City of the British Empire today." King Jean looked back at the privy council. *"We go to war!"* continued King Jean.

"Your Excellency, when we heard word this morning of the attack on the British Empire, we took the initiative in your absence to recall the army and prepare the navy to sail, if that is what your excellency wished?" said the privy councillor.

King Jean clapped his hands together in celebration and began to walk between the privy council towards the doors they entered through. *"You've done well, men, very well. Come! All of you."* King Jean stopped for a moment and looked back at Camila and Harriet with a smile while motioning with a nod of his head toward the wooden doors. *"If you thought the sphere was fun, I believe this will excite you both a little more! Even you Lady Kerr,"* continued the King as his laughed echoed through the hangar. Camila and Harriet followed King Jean through the wooden doors with the privy council close behind, still marching in perfect synchronisation.

As the King led them through a series of curving corridors, the line of fire light followed them on either side of the white stone ground sensing their every turn lighting the way until they were faced with another set of wooden doors but this time much bigger than the ones they came through in the hangar. The line of fire crept up either side of the doors along the wall until they filled two small glass spheres with the fire light. King Jean placed his right hand in the centre of the large square wooden doors and in an instant, with a crack followed by a load creak the doors flung open. The fire light leapt from the spheres and into this new huge circular room creeping along the walls until the fire filled ore glass spheres on the curved wall, giving light to the entire room.

The King shuffled his way into the room followed closely by Camila, Harriet and the privy council.

"Here... this is where we board the ships." The king pointed to a large circular hole in the ground edged with square black slate. Harriet moved forward ahead of the group, squaring her eyes at the hole in the ground.

"This is similar to our Passing Arches in the Imperial City," said Harriet softly as King Jean nodded.

"Correct! We call them Slipway Tunnels. They work along the same lines as your Passing Arches. This Tunnel connects directly to my navy's flagship. If you two would follow me *through we can get underway."* The King beckoned Camila and Harriet towards the Slipway Tunnel with his boney and frail hand. *"My privy, you will stay here. If we fail... well... that means I am dead most likely, so the Kingdom will be yours to find a successor!"* King Jean continued. his voice chuckled with a hint of sarcasm as each of the privy councillors exchanged bemused looks. King Jean joined Camila and Harriet at the edge of the Slipway Tunnel. Camila frowned as she looked at the King, clearly disapproving of his behaviour towards the privy council.

"Oh, silly girl. I am only playing with them. I have made the appropriate arrangements in case of my demise. But at my age, you've got to have a little fun whenever you can! Advice I think you should adhere to, Lady Kerr," said King Jean in a patronising manner that made Camila fidget with irritation. She shook her head slightly as if to brush off her anger and peered down into the Slipway Tunnel. Just like the Passing Arches within the Passing Dome, the hole was blanketed with a dark grey mist that flowed out past the edges covering their feet. Camila narrowed her eyes as she looked down and then moved her gaze to the King.

"So? We just step in?" asked Camila.

King Jean smiled and placed his left foot hovering over the hole. *"Oui! We fall to the ship,"* said King Jean and then he placed his right hand behind Camila and without warning, he pushed her into the hole. As she fell forward, she tried to spin round and grab onto the King's robe but he had stepped back out of her reach and she fell deeply and disappeared through the Slipway Tunnel's mist.

"*Ha ha ha! Bon voyage, Lady Kerr! It is our turn now!*" said King Jean looking at Harriet, whose mouth was a gasp and in pure shock at what the King had done but she had no time to express herself verbally as the King had unsteadily leapt into the hole behind Camila leaving just Harriet in the room on her own with the privy council.

Her body trembling with fear, she took a step forward, her tip toes hanging over the edge. She closed her eyes and lent forward, falling into the hole. She could feel the familiar cold dampness of the mist engulf her body but then she went completely weightless. There was no feeling of falling but she didn't feel still either. Within moments her feet had grounded to something solid and she could hear the lapping of water and the smell of salty air. Her eyes were still closed as tightly as possible, her head still shaking with fear.

"*Harriet! Open your eyes. It's okay,*" said Camila.

Harriet could feel Camila's hand on her arm softly reassuring her as she opened her eyes. After a few seconds of her eyes adjusting to the light from the darkness she came from, she started to make out the shapes and colours surrounding her. She steadied herself from the soft back-and-forth, side-to-side motion of the ship on water. The decks and masts of the ship were all made of a polished bronze type of metal that glistened in the bright sunlight. She looked up at the sails which were like no sails she had ever seen before, an almost transparent, silk-like sparkling material that rippled in the wind. King Jean walked up next to Harriet, smiling softly.

"Remarkable, no?" he said, while motioning with his hand to the port-side of the ship where over a dozen more ships of the same polished bronze-like configuration lay.

Each had three gigantic gun turrets mounted at the front ready for battle. Camila looked at Harriet, her lips pursed. *"I don't like the way he did it either but we are here with a navy, Harriet – just like Jacob and the Queen asked. Now we can finally help him take back our city,"* said Camila sternly and confidently. Harriet nodded her head and reached out to hold the deck bannister to steady herself.

"At least we are going home!" said Harriet, her voice warbling heavily, *"and I hope you don't mind me saying my lady but… the least time I can spend with that man, the better,"* Harriet continued, as she looked at King Jean. Camila simply chuckled as the sea air blew her golden hair across her face. She reached into her dirtied and torn robe pocket and pulled out a piece of white parchment. Harriet stepped forward next to Camila, looking down at the blank parchment

"Is that MagiChartam?" asked Harriet.

Camila looked at Harriet and smiled, *"Yes, it is. It links directly to my office in the Royal Palace,"* said Camila as she placed her finger on the MagiChartam parchment and began to write.

Prince Jacob, we are coming. Camila.

The words burned bright with a blue sparkling light as she wrote and then disappeared with a light misty smoke, dissipating in the air, leaving the parchment blank once again.

"At least now the Prince will know we are coming. Let's hope it's not too late," continued Camila as she looked out across the horizon, her eyes focused and her mission clear.

CHAPTER FIVE

RETURN TO THE WHITE ISLANDS

"*Well… here we are again!*" said Elliot, dressed in a dark flowing robe that trailed a little behind him as he looked up at the Passing Dome's curved glass ceiling and then at the countless Passing Arches suspended in mid-air throughout the Dome, but none of them had the shimmering light like before; this time, the arches lay still and dark. Behind Elliot were six of the best and most powerful Imperial Guards dressed in their impeccably tailored green robes and silver helmets with olden Wielding Spears at their sides. Their eyes were locked forward and backs perfectly straight; they waited for Elliot's command.

Smiling at Elliot, Jacob, in a lengthy dark robe with silver-plated armour hugging his chest and torso, stood a few paces to his side with the Caretaker's son, a short and plump man with greying facial stubble and short hair.

"*Except, this time, we are going separate ways. I've had Lennard here, the Caretaker's son, disable all of the Passing Arches except for the ones we are about to use to the White Islands, Colghorn and your one,*" Jacob pointed to the archway nearest Elliot, "*which leads to the cove on the beach below the entrance to Parliament House at Dover Cliff. Hopefully the members of Parliament will be safely inside. They'll only lift the Sealing Ward once they see your Royal Seal. Once you're inside, get them out and bring them back here before Thomas finds them himself. Meanwhile I will do the prisoner exchange on the White Islands. Now... Lennard if you could open the Passing Arch to Colghorn, please? The guards there should be ready with Neville,*" continued Jacob as Lennard nodded. He took a few paces forward and then summoned an air spell lifting high up into the air toward the Colghorn Passing Archway which had been moved since the battle to the higher most secure archways at the top of the Dome. As Lennard drifted out of sight, hurried footsteps came from behind Jacob and Elliot from the Passing Dome entrance, causing them to look back.

"*Lord Elliot!*" shouted the single Imperial Guard rushing towards Elliot with a piece of parchment in his hand. Jacob frowned at Elliot, a little confused, as the guard handed the parchment to him.

"*Thank you, William*" said Elliot as he looked down and read the MagiChartam. Elliot smiled and then traced his finger along the parchment with the familiar blue sparkling light followed by the misty smoke as the words disappeared. He folded the paper and handed it back to the guard, William. "*And no one else has seen this, William?*" asked Elliot, his bright blue eyes staring straight at William.

"*No, my lord. As you commanded, any word from Lady Kerr is to be brought to you or King Jacob and no one else,*" replied William. "*Thank you, you may return to your station, William,*" and with Elliot's command, William rushed back.

Jacob walked over closer to Elliot and tilted his head, eyebrows raised. "*Word from Camila?*" said Jacob, slightly irritated.

"*Look, don't be mad but I placed William on Camila's personal guard duty for when she returns, knowing that any word from her would be sent to her private office and he would be the first to see it. I know you trust the Royal Council but there's something that doesn't sit right with me about Lady Black... so I had William keep any correspondence from Camila limited to our eyes only,*" said Elliot, trying his best to seem confident in his decision. Jacob nodded slowly and then looked back towards the Dome entrance.

"*What did she say?*" asked Jacob submissively. Elliot smiled and clapped his hands together with a tilt of his head.

"*She is on her way with the French King and his navy!*" replied Elliot as Jacob let out a huge sigh of relief, his shoulders visibly relaxing. *"That is great news,"* said Jacob who was now looking back up towards the Colghorn Passing Arch as four figures were now floating back down towards them. Elliot followed Jacob's gaze as Jacob frowned; he remembered Elliot had written something back to Camila before he handed the MagiChartam back to the guard. Jacob looked down and then over at Elliot. *"What did you write back to Camila?"* Jacob asked. Elliot looked at Jacob warmly and directly into his eyes.

"Something you would not agree with but something you will have to trust me on," replied Elliot as Jacob's frown deepened. He opened his mouth to protest to Elliot but stopped short for Jacob did trust Elliot and he knew if he was keeping something from him then it was for the right reasons, so Jacob simply nodded and looked back up at the figures now getting closer to them from the Colghorn Passing Arch.

The four figures had now floated down to the ground in front of Jacob and Elliot. Lennard was now accompanied by two Imperial Guards and Neville. The guards' spears pointed at Neville's neck as they forced him to kneel before Jacob, his hands tied behind him with a powerful binding spell.

The dark haired and muscular Neville now had some short stubble on his face which had obviously grown during his imprisonment in Colghorn. His deep dark eyes looked up and locked with Jacob's. *"I won't tell you anything, Jacob. You're wasting your time,"* said Neville and then he looked down at the ground.

"It's a good thing I haven't brought you here to talk then, isn't it!" replied Jacob. Neville looked back up at Jacob and then around the Dome, taking in Elliot and his company of guards.

"What's going on then? We're in the Dome. Where are you taking me?" snarled Neville.

Jacob motioned his hand up high towards the White Islands archway. "*Home, Neville. Your wife and mother-in-law have agreed to a prisoner exchange,*" replied Jacob as Neville's face turned to shock. "*Not possible. Catherine would never agree to it,*" spat Neville.

"Apparently she has. Shall we?" said Jacob as he looked at Lennard and the guards standing by Neville. All three nodded as Jacob stepped forward closer to the guards, Neville and Lennard readying themselves to be lifted up to the White Islands archway. Elliot moved forward and grabbed Jacob's arm, looking into his eyes. "*Please be careful,*" Elliot pleaded.

Jacob nodded and smiled. "*You as well. Get back here as soon as you can. Once we are back here and with the French navy at our heels, we will take back the city and the country,*" Jacob said with pure confidence. Elliot nodded and let go of Jacob's arm so he could join the rest of them floating upwards to the White Islands archway. Lennard looked back down at Elliot and shouted, "*I will come back down to take you to the Dover Cliff arch, Lord Elliot,*" and then the five of them quickly ascended disappearing out of Elliot's sight.

Jacob kept looking down at Elliot until the stone ground entry to the White Islands archway appeared underneath his feet. He looked up to see the Passing Arch had lit up with the shimmering light ready for them to pass through. Lennard raised his hand out to motion them through. Jacob stepped forward past the guards and Neville and walked through the shimmering light of the Passing Arch. The guards ushered Neville through behind him and then they too passed through.

CHAPTER SIX

AN UNEXPECTED CONDITION

❖

    Jacob had appeared in an instant on the other side of the Passing Arch in the corner of the Regent's Hall estate, closely followed by the guards and Neville. The salty sea air had once again filled Jacob's lungs as he looked up at clear blue sky and sun shining brightly over the Regent's Hall ahead of him. Coming down the pathway flanked by two soldiers dressed in weathered leather uniforms was the Lady Regent Catherine of the White Islands and behind her was Prince Johnathan being dragged in chains by three of the dungeon guards, including Tom. As they drew closer, Jacob could see that his father had been beaten and the anger within Jacob began to grow but something started to distract him. His mind began to fog and a voice, ever so faint, was starting to etch into his mind. He tilted his head at first trying to fight it but then he began to recognise the presence that was entering his mind which made Jacob relax and allow the voice in.

"Son, I can't hold this for long. Kendra and her son are using a masking spell to hide next to the passing arch. They must come home with us. I can't explain – trust me."

Jacob's father had lost the connection to his mind and he managed to shake off the disorientation quickly enough before anyone had noticed. Catherine had stopped just in front of Jacob wearing a long dark grey fur robe as she leant to one side glancing a look at Neville and pursing her lips tightly. She then looked back at the prisoner guards holding Johnathan and twitched her head to motion to them to bring him forward. Jacob responded by doing the same to the Imperial Guards holding Neville.

Both sides brought their prisoners forward in a neutral spot between Catherine and Jacob.

"I have not agreed to this lightly, King Jacob. My daughter was insistent that she gets her husband back and my grandson his father," said Catherine in a high shrill voice.

Neville looked up and around as if searching for something. *"Where is Kendra?"* he asked desperately. Catherine pointed back to the Regent's Hall; the weathered battered grey stone walls showed the signs of neglect like most of the buildings on Farland Island.

"She waits for you at the Hall, Neville. Her presence would only be a distraction. Now… let's get on with it," said Catherine pointing to Johnathan and Neville.

"*Make the switch,*" commanded Jacob.

The three dungeon guards released the chains holding Johnathan and the Imperial Guards lifted back their spears and, holding them by their sides, released Neville who stood up from his kneeling position and began to walk unsteadily towards Catherine as Johnathan limped towards Jacob until they passed each other, exchanging a brief glance between them and a nod. Johnathan joined Jacob at his side as they smiled at each other.

"*King Jacob?*" said Johnathan with a slight chuckle; Jacob nodded and twisted his head backward towards the Passing Arch motioning his father there. Johnathan, now being aided by the Imperial Guards, limped to the archway as Jacob looked back at Catherine his eyes narrowing.

"*Then we are done, Lady Regent?*" said Jacob sternly.

"*We are,*" Catherine replied returning his narrow-eyed stare and then she began to turn away waving at her guards to follow.

"*Then we depart as enemies, Catherine? Is there no hope for us, the Empire and the Islands?*" shouted Jacob as Catherine stopped and twisted her head back around to look at Jacob.

"Your optimism is unfounded. Be happy this happened without incident, Your Majesty," snarled Catherine.

Jacob bowed his head down and was about to turn away and join his father and the guards at the Passing Arch but out of nowhere the loudest crack of the sound barrier being broken high above them caused everyone to stop and look up. A figure, flying through the air, leaving a darkened trail, scarred the blue sky above. Jacob looked back down at Catherine who was trying to look at the sky by shielding the sunlight with her hand.

"You told him?" Jacob bellowed at Catherine who was shaking her head and her mouth open wide. She looked confused and then they both looked back up at the sky as the figure came hurtling towards them smashing into the ground causing it to ripple and explode towards Jacob who summoned a barrier spell just in time to protect him, his father and the guards behind from the debris flying through the air. As the dust and debris settled, the figure that had landed in between him and Catherine began to come into focus. The hooded figure was kneeling from the impact and began to stand upright, staring at Jacob who could see the flash of pale green eyes underneath the dark hood.

"Thomas..." Jacob said quietly but Thomas didn't hesitate a moment. Throwing his arms wide, palms out, he summoned waters spells, gathering the oceans on either side of the island towards him in fluid spirals of rushing water into a sphere a few feet above him. Jacob reacted just as quickly closing his eyes and focusing all of his magic between his palms in front of his navel summoning the most powerful

fire spell he could muster. Within milliseconds, a sphere of fire equalling Thomas's water spell had formed. The two locked eyes for a second, which felt like minutes to Jacob, until they both projected the streams of fire and water towards each other. Both spells clashed together, the brightness of the fire and the spray of the water splintering off in random directions as the two met. The sizzling sounds of the water hitting the fire was as loud as the rushing of the water. At first the two spells were matched, neither one gaining more ground over the other, but Jacob could sense that Thomas's magic was weaker than the last night they fought above the palace. He didn't waste any time wondering why this was but instead he took advantage of the weakness and began to transform his fire spell into a lightning spell. In an instant Jacob's fire spell morphed into lightning, taking Thomas completely by surprise which enabled the electricity to flow and conduct through Thomas's water spell until the bolts struck him squarely in the chest, sending Thomas hurtling backwards through the air, striking the hard stone circular wall surrounding the Regent's estate. He fell to the ground, landing on his hands and knees, spitting out blood. He looked back up at Jacob, his eyes bright green with fury and his skin pale and drained from the fight. Jacob turned back around and ran to the archway.

"QUICKLY! THROUGH THE ARCHWAY!" Jacob shouted as he caught up with his father and the guards. They ran together towards the archway but just as they were merely feet away from the stone archway, Thomas had composed himself and summered a splintering lightning spell striking the archway on multiple points, shattering the stone and collapsing the Passing Arch. As the lightning spell bounced off the arch, it struck the nearby area destroying the masking spell that was concealing Kendra and her baby son from everyone else. The impact from the spell forced them all to the ground shielding their faces. Jacob, struggling to get to his feet, looked back at Thomas who was now completely exhausted from the magic he had summoned and was struggling to keep consciousness. As he fell back to his knees, he looked over towards Catherine and shouted with the last of his energy.

"*TAKE THEM!*" As the words left Thomas's mouth, he fell backwards unconscious. Catherine looked over at Jacob who was back to his feet but the rest of them, including Kendra and her son, were still on the ground. Neville, who was now rushing forward next to Catherine, stared at Kendra his face in pure confusion.

Even though her ears were still ringing from the loudness of the lightning spell that struck the arch, she could read Neville's lips and the words he was mouthing. *"What are you doing?"* said Neville. Kendra shook her head as tears rolled down her face; she looked down at her son who thankfully was unharmed from the shards of stone that flew through the air from the arch.

"*GUARDS! TAKE THEM DOWN! AND BRING MY DAUGHTER TO ME NOW!*" bellowed Catherine. The Island guards nervously looked at each other as more guards came running down from the Regent's Hall, all of them summoning spells of fire and air as Jacob looked over at Thomas's unconscious body and then began to summon another barrier spell to protect them from the next attack from the guards but, from behind him, over thirty soldiers dressed in all-white perfectly tailored uniforms and helmets came flying overhead sending fire spells into the Islands guards followed by the whooshing sounds of cannons striking the Regent's Hall walls and exploding in a fiery mass of stone and soil. Jacob, perplexed by the turn of events, heard a thud from behind him; as he turned round, ready for anything, he came face to face with Camila. Jacob shook his head in surprise.

"Camila! What in the Queen's name are you doing here?" Jacob said, unaware that the volume of his voice was a little below shouting.

"Elliot," replied Camila simply. Jacob tilted his head and looked up at the sky with a smile. *"He never does as he's told, does he!?"* said Jacob laughing.

"No! Thankfully! Quickly, the French are waiting for us. Can you summon an air spell big enough to get us to the ships?" asked Camila.

Jacob nodded confidently and motioned his father, the guards, Kendra and her son to gather round him and Camila who looked at Kendra and the baby with confusion and then looked at Jacob for an explanation.
"You'll have to ask my father about that!" said Jacob as he looked over at Catherine and her guards who were dragging Neville back to the Regent's Hall, shouting Kendra's name and reaching out with his hands for her.

"MY SON? KENDRA!" Jacob frowned and unsure of what was happening shook off the feeling and summoned the air

spell lifting them all high into the air above the Island. The French soldiers quickly flew to their side, encircling them to protect from any further attacks.

Camila pointed towards the horizon where Jacob could see three bronze-coloured French battle ships just off the coast of the Island. Two of the French ships were attacking the lone American Republic ship which was attempting to flee, successfully evading their cannon fire using the huge jagged quartz-coloured rocks surrounding Farland Island as cover. Now being guided by the French soldiers, Jacob flew them towards the largest of the three French ships which was still sending cannon fire towards the Regent's Hall. Camila, who was just off Jacob's left shoulder, shouted to him over the whooshing wind as they flew, *"THAT'S KING JEAN'S SHIP!"*

Jacob gave a heavy nod as they flew quickly through the air arriving a few hundred feet above King Jean's ship. The cannons fired rapidly and relentlessly at Farland Island, with each shot leaving a trail of dark smoke in their wake. They began to float down towards the ship's bright bronze deck where the elderly figure of King Jean stood looking up at them as they lowered and met the deck floor. Jacob, exhausted from the magical exertion, was happy his feet were back on solid ground. His hands on his knees with his back bent over slightly he looked up at the French King and smiled.

"King Jean! It's bloody good to see you," Jacob said breathlessly. King Jean closed his eyes slowly and returned Jacob's smile with a singular nod of his head.

"You all look tired and hungry. This way," said King Jean as he motioned them towards a large bronze-metal looking hatchway that led to a cabin underneath the upper ship's deck where the cannons still fired upon the Island.

Jacob looked at his father, Kendra and her baby son who all looked tired with the baby crying loudly, no doubt in protest at the loud cannon fire. Jacob nodded at King Jean and began to walk slowly towards the cabin.

"Thank you, Your Majesty, but we must leave here at once. Thomas Colet is on the Island. We fought and he is unconscious but when he wakes, he will be powerful enough to be a threat to you and your ships," said Jacob as they stood at the threshold of the cabin doorway.

King Jean raised his bushy white eyebrows and nodded slowly and then turned his head towards a tall man dressed in a tight-fitted white naval uniform with eight silver stripes around his waist.

"Admiral, get us away from here at best speed. We must rejoin the fleet heading to the Imperial City," ordered the King.

The Captain hurried off and quickly shouted his orders to the crew. King Jean and Jacob looked at Kendra and her baby who were disappearing into the darkness of the cabin. King Jean glanced slightly at Jacob who could feel his stare.

"*There's a few more of you than I thought we'd be picking up, Your Highness,*" said King Jean. Jacob sighed and nodded softly. "*Always the unexpected when my father is involved.*"

CHAPTER SEVEN

FATHER AND SON REUNITED

❖

Jacob and King Jean entered the warmly lit cabin joining Prince Johnathan, Camila, Harriet, Kendra and the baby who was nestled neatly in a light blue blanket cooing from his mother's embrace. The cabin's walls were covered in the same bronze surface as the exterior of the ship. The shimmering surface reflected the fire light coming from the small glass spheres in the corners of the cabin. White oak wood and fabric-studded chairs were placed lavishly in a large circle facing inward towards an open fire encased in a bronze half dome floating a few inches above the deck. There was a light knock on the cabin door entrance.

"*Come,*" wheezed King Jean.

Crewmen opened the cabin doors carrying plates of food. Cured meats and cheese were brought in and placed on a long table at the corner of the room with plenty of water, ice and what looked like wine to Jacob's eye.

"Thank you. Please leave us." ordered King Jean and the crewmen left at once closing the doors behind them shutting out the sounds of crashing waves and shouting from the deckhands and officers outside.

"Please eat and sit," said King Jean as he motioned his hands towards the food and chairs. Jacob walked over to Camila who was brushing down her robes and adjusting her hair from the salty wind.

"Camila! How did you get here so fast? We only just had word from you that you were on your way," asked Jacob. Camila looked over at King Jean and then back at Jacob.

"These ships are incredible, Your Highness, far superior to anything we or anyone else has in their navy," said Camila.

"It's the sails! A new design from our constructers. The fabric is woven with a wind containment spell and then another spell amplifies its power one hundred-fold before it's released," boasted King Jean.

"Very impressive, Your Majesty. Thank you for coming to our aid. The British Empire is in dire need of it," said Jacob as he sat down in one of the fabric-studded chairs. King Jean sat down opposite and placed his hands together looking at Jacob.

"Of course. This Thomas Colet must be stopped. It's in all our interests, no?" said King Jean softly.

Jacob nodded and then looked over at his father who was now sitting down, with Kendra and her baby standing just behind him. Jacob frowned and looked at his father with a narrowed gaze.

"Would anyone care to explain why we have the Lady Regent's daughter and grandson with us?" asked Jacob.

Johnathan twisted his head back to look at Kendra briefly and then return his son's gaze. "*I think that is something you, Kendra and I should discuss privately,*" replied Johnathan.

Jacob's frown deepened slightly showing a hint of impatience but nodded as he looked at Kendra.

"*It appears your mother didn't honour our agreement, Kendra. Thomas knew about the exchange. You assured me this would be done without his knowledge!*" said Jacob, unable to hide his anger.

Kendra shook her head vigorously in protest "*No! She wouldn't! She did NOT! My mother is many things but she would never go back on her word to me. If Thomas knew you were going to be there, it was not her doing!*" Kendra's voice shook in defence of her mother.

Jacob leant back in his chair, his face relaxing and eyes darting around the room in thought. Camila stepped forward to sit down next to Jacob and caught his eye.

"Then who else knew you were coming here?" asked Camila. Jacob looked at her with one eyebrow raised slightly.

"Elliot… and…" Jacob looked out of the window at the end of the cabin, the waves crashing up and ocean water spraying upwards blocking out the last of the sun as it set over the horizon.

"And?" Camila said, pressing Jacob to continue. Jacob's frown returned to his face as he looked back at Camila.

"And Lady Black," continued Jacob as he thought back to his last conversation with Elliot and then it dawned on him what else she and only she knew. Jacob stood up at once and looked at King Jean.

"Your Majesty, we have to change course at once!" pleaded Jacob as King Jean raised slowly from his chair looking at Jacob.

"Change course? But I thought the Imperial City —?" Jacob cut the King off "No, no, we have to get to Elliot NOW! Dover Cliff. As quickly as possible!" Jacob said, panicked. King Jean nodded quickly.

"Very well. The coordinates?" asked King Jean as he made his way back to the cabin doors.

"Lady Kerr knows the location. Camila, would you go with him," said Jacob. Camila got up from her chair in an instant and tapped Harriet on the shoulder who was nibbling at some cheese.

"Of course! Come Harriet, we must give them some privacy," said Camila, nodding her head towards Jacob, Johnathan and Kendra. Harriet wiped down her mouth, straightened her robe and started to walk towards the cabin door with Camila but stopped just short next to Jacob and looked down at him with her eyes glassing over.

"Your Highness, I'm sorry to ask but my son? Lennard? Is he —?" Harriet asked as Jacob placed both his hands on hers and smiled, cutting her off mid-sentence.

"Alive and well. He's doing a fine job of looking after the Passing Dome in your absence," said Jacob as Harriet let out a huge sigh of relief and continued on with Camila and King Jean, exiting the cabin leaving Jacob alone with his father, Kendra and her baby.

"So?" Jacob said, raising both his hands in the air, looking at his father and Kendra who still stood standing behind Johnathan, "can you tell me how you came to be here, Kendra?" continued Jacob speaking softly as he was acutely aware that she felt shaken at this moment.

"I… I asked your father for asylum for my son and I. He said you'd agree," Kendra replied, her voice quiet but clear.

Jacob looked at his father, tilting his head slightly. *"Once he knew why, yes... I said you'd agree,"* said Johnathan, tilting his head towards Jacob

"And the why is?... I am waiting with bated breath here," queried Jacob, now looking at both of them.

Kendra looked down at her baby and then at Jacob, her mouth open but no words came. Johnathan looked back up at her and breathed in deeply.

"It's the boy. She wants him away from his father for fear of what he might do and the man he has become... is that about it?" Johnathan said looking at Kendra for approval who nodded and then walked over to sit in the vacant chair next to him, holding her baby close, *"and the father is what makes this so interesting,"* continued Johnathan as Jacob narrowed his eyes at Kendra, shaking his head very slightly.

"Then why would you work so hard to convince your mother to do the prisoner exchange if you fear Neville so? We had him locked up in Colghorn a world away from you," asked Jacob. Johnathan leaned forward looking intensely at Jacob through the flames of the open fire.

"Because, son... Neville isn't the father," revealed Johnathan, *"the father is T—!"*

"Thomas... it is Thomas," said Kendra cutting Johnathan off, her voice submissive as she brushed her thumb across the baby's face. Jacob's back bolted upright, his eyes wide removing any trace of the tiredness he felt.

"Thomas? Thomas Colet? The King of the Dark Knights is that baby's father?" blurted out Jacob in disbelief. Kendra looked up at Jacob, her face plain and showing no signs of expression.

"So, you see why we had to flee. That is not the future I want for my son," said Kendra, her tone flat and quiet.

"And Thomas knows?" asked Jacob.

Kendra shook her head. "No. And Neville believes the boy is his," replied Kendra.

Jacob rubbed his chin in thought, staring down at the bronze deck floor.

"Thomas has to know. His magic is powerful in ways I didn't think possible. He would sense the child was his," said Jacob.

Kendra continued to shake her head. "Today was the first time I've seen him since we… since he was last on the Island," said Kendra.

"I see. Poor Neville… it'll destroy him when he finds out," stated Jacob. Kendra frowned deeply at Jacob.

"Surely it's better for Neville, and the rest of our world come to that, to believe the he is the father?" said Kendra looking at both Johnathan and Jacob.

"Probably, Kendra, but secrets like these, especially when it involves people like Thomas, they tend to have a way of coming to light at the worst times. But I agree, for now and for the baby's sake, his parentage should be kept as the world believes it to be," Jacob said as he stood up and walked over to Kendra and knelt down in front of her looking at the baby smiling and then up at her.

"I understand why you did what you did and how hard that must've been for you. My father did the right thing agreeing to this. We will, of course, grant you asylum. I guess that's one of the perks of being a King now… I get to help people no matter how tiny they are," continued Jacob as he looked back down at the baby. "What's his name?" asked Jacob as Kendra looked down at her baby, a single tear falling from her eye and landing on the baby's cheek.

"I haven't been able to bring myself to name him yet. I don't know why," replied Kendra.

Jacob placed his hand on her arm. "When the time is right, the right name will come and a fine name I am sure it will be. I suggest you and the baby get some rest. I'd imagine the crew here have organised some kind of rooms or quarters for us," said Jacob.

Kendra nodded softly, stood up and made her way back towards the cabin doors. She looked back at Jacob and Johnathan as she opened the door. "Thank you," she said to them and left, closing the door behind her. Jacob sat down in her chair opposite his father. Johnathan placed his hand on Jacob's knee and smiled.

"King Jacob eh?!" said Johnathan, as Jacob laughed.

"Only while mother recovers! Then she can gladly take the crown back," replied Jacob. Johnathan's expression changed to a stern worried look.

"Your mother? How is she?" asked Johnathan. "I've only been told bits from the prison guard and Kendra," he continued.

"She's alive and safe at the Royal Palace but unconscious after the battle with Thomas. She was incredible, father." Jacob's face lit up with pride that Johnathan was very pleased to see on his son's face. "The power she had summoned to fight him… I didn't think it was possible and far beyond anything I've achieved. And the same goes for Thomas, if I'm honest… the abilities he possessed during that fight scared me, which eventually were too much for mother to fend off," Jacob continued as he looked down at the deck floor remembering the moments he had with his mother onboard The Sabre. The regret he felt from pulling his hand away from her was still raw and he wished with his life that would not be their last moment.

Johnathan sensed his son was in pain and got up from his chair and threw his arms around Jacob, startling him. "She is so proud of you, son. We both are. And don't put yourself down; you've faced Thomas yourself and come away with your life," said Johnathan proudly as let go of his son and leant back into his chair, Jacob smiling at him warmly.

"Maybe. But he was a lot weaker today than when I faced him above the Palace and that was even after his fight with mother which would have wakened him for sure. I don't know… maybe he is still recovering from that; either way, he wasn't at full power and I don't think I could defeat him if he were, at least not on my own," replied Jacob as his mind drifted to Elliot, hoping that this French ship he was on would arrive at Dover Cliff before Thomas or his forces.

"If Kendra speaks the truth and her mother didn't sell us out to Thomas, then it would appear Elliot's suspicions of Lady Black could be well founded, which makes me worry about whether she has turned any more of the Royal Council against us," said Jacob.

"And your mother's safety at the Palace as well?" said Johnathan, with a more worried look on his face. Jacob shook his head.

"No, she will be fine. I placed my most trusted personal guards to protect her while I was gone. Not even the Royal Council are permitted to enter; again, that is something Elliot insisted on before we left," replied Jacob confidently.

"You said she's unconscious? This is from a spell that Thomas summoned against her no doubt. I take it you've tried to reach her with mind spells?" queried Johnathan.

"Yes, of course I tried but… I can't explain it; every time I've tried to reach her, it felt like she wasn't there. I don't mean empty, but… like she was elsewhere." Jacob shook his head, trying to find the words to explain to his father who had got up to put some ice from the drinks table into a cloth and placed it on his swollen eye before returning to his chair.

"When you faced Thomas today... Did you feel anything different?" Johnathan asked as he dabbed his eye with the ice.

"There was something, a feeling of sorts... but I shook it off. Why?" replied Jacob, confused.

"Did it feel like a presence?" Johnathan pressed.

"Possibly, I actually thought it was you trying to speak to me again with a mind spell. It had the same feel to it. Do you think it's significant?" asked Jacob, who now was genuinely intrigued where his father was going with this.

"It's a theory. A wild one at that but given what you have told me about your mother's condition and Thomas's weakness since... it's possible your mother is still in the fight." Jacob leant forwards in his chair, perplexed at what his father had just said.

"Still in the fight how?" asked Jacob.

"MagiPower Projection," Johnathan said with a hint of a chuckle behind his words.

"What even is that?" laughed Jacob.

"Something your mother was obsessed with a very long time ago. Her and her friend Otyre, when they were teenagers, used to sneak out of the Palace and practice what she called, projection spells. I, of course, was widely jealous of Otyre and the time he was spending with her so I used to follow them. They had found a way to completely control the magical force within their body and well... there's no better way to say this than, they left their bodies and travelled as their magical force. Fascinated myself, I did what I always do... I rummaged through the ancient libraries and learnt everything I could that told me more about what they had discovered. It turned that our people had a name for it, MagiPower Projection, and I also learnt it was forbidden to practice it because it was so dangerous. The temptation to travel further and further and manipulate their magical power beyond the law of MagiNature was fatal to almost everyone that had tried to push that boundary before them. Of course, as soon as I leant this I feared for your mother's life and rushed to find the both of them." Johnathan's eyes stared into the memories of his past as Jacob studied his father's face.

"Mother never mentioned this Otyre to me before. Where is he now?" asked Jacob. Johnathan shook his head, snapping his gaze back to Jacob.

"She never speaks of it or him... it's too painful for her. You see, when I went to find them that day, they were in the middle of this MagiPower Projection spell but something had gone wrong. Otyre was awake but your mother was lifeless and completely unresponsive to anything we could do to wake her. She had pushed too hard and tried to manipulate more of her magic than she understood. So Otyre, in a desperate attempt, found a way to use his MagiPower to project, linking himself with her and attempting to pull her back. Obviously, it worked and she woke up and was alive but at a terrible cost... Otyre never returned. Without its MagiPower his body died eventually. Your mother was broken after this. She swore to me that she'd never perform that kind of magic again," replied Johnathan, as Jacob was lost in deep thought. He started to understand what his father was alluding too.

"So… you think it's possible that she did this MagiPower Projection and then what? Somehow contained Thomas's power?" said Jacob not believing his own words.

"What I know… is that she knew you were the only person in the Empire, or world for that matter, that is even close to her ability and power. If she could do anything to give you a fighting chance to win against Thomas she would, without hesitation, especially if she knew she was about to be defeated." Johnathan's voice was full of confidence and emotion. Jacob flicked his eyebrows high and then frowned deeply towards his father.

"If all this, quite frankly, battiness is true and she is still in the fight like you say… then I hope you can figure a way out to brining her back, father. That is your area of expertise after all, creating spells," demanded Jacob.

"Even though your mother promised me she'd never use that kind of magic again, I knew I needed to be prepared if she or someone else tried. So, I studied MagiPower Projection and a few years ago, I think I came up with a way to do what Otyre did safely. But I need the books in the Imperial Library at the Palace to do it but that's not the hardest bit… your mother and Thomas will have to be near each other for me to do the spell," said Johnathan. Jacob nodded slowly.

"Well… then we will just have to figure that one out on the go, won't we?" replied Jacob. Johnathan looked directly into Jacob's eyes as one side of his lips curled into a half smile.

"So… I've been gone for three days and my son is King, my wife is possibly performing forbidden magic in her sleep and there's an alleged traitor in the Royal Council. Anything else I've missed?" continued Johnathan as he chuckled at Jacob.

Jacob laughed softly and tilted his head to one side briefly while still looking at his father.

"Well… I suppose me being married is newsworthy?" Jacob said smiling, waiting for his father's reaction which came quickly and loudly.

"WHAT? *Jacob my son! Finally!*" Johnathan rejoiced as he stood up and pulled Jacob out of his chair by his arms and hugged him tightly. Jacob laughed as his eyes glassed over with happiness at his father's reaction.

"Ha ha, thank you, father," said Jacob as Johnathan let go of him and took a step back, throwing his iced cloth to the floor. He looked at his son proudly.

"And what took you so long, eh?" Johnathan asked.

"Suppose I was just waiting for the right national crises to get the romance flowing!" replied Jacob laughing with his father.

"Well then. I hope this ship is as fast as the King claims. I need to see my son-in-law!" Johnathan said as he looked out of the window, the waves still crashing and spraying water on the glass.

CHAPTER EIGHT

DOVER CLIFF

❖

After just a few hours rest Jacob and Johnathan had been called back to the ship's deck outside. The water had calmed, the night air was still and the moon hung low over the horizon. The ship's sails had been pulled in and Jacob could feel by the lack of wind on his face that they had come to a stop. Jacob and his father walked towards Camila and King Jean who stood side by side on the upper deck at the front of the ship looking through a long telescope. As Jacob climbed the stairs to the upper front deck, his father behind him, he looked out to where the telescope was pointed. The moonlight brushed the steep white long cliffs of Dover in an almost sparkling sliver light. The light sparkles bounced off the rippling ocean beneath the ship and glistened on the hull. Jacob's robes fluttered in the light winds showing his silver armour around his torso, catching the moonlight as he turned to face Camila who was pointing towards the cliffs.

"The entrance to Parliament House. It's open," said Camila gravely.

She placed her hand on the telescope and motioned Jacob to look through. He placed his eye over the brass eyepiece and tried to focus on what he was seeing. Half way up, the steepest cliff was a darkened hole about three metres high, plain to see in contrast with the rest of the whiteness of the cliff. Camila was right, the tunnel entrance had been opened but more importantly, the masking spells around it were completely disabled. Jacob pulled back from the telescope and looked at Camila and King Jean, who was dressed in a thick fluffy grey robe with his hood up over his head.

"The masking spells are gone?" asked Jacob.

"Yes, but that's not all. This telescope can also show us only what humans see. The masking spell to hide the entrance from the humans is gone too," replied Camila as she looked out at the cliffs.

"We have to get in there now. Your Majesty… could I call upon your generosity once again to send some of your guards with me into the cliff?" Jacob asked desperately. The King bowed his head slowly and then waved his hand towards the guards standing behind him.

"Take them. They are my personal guard and they are my best," replied the King as the four guards stood to attention and then marched forwards to Jacob. Three of them, men dressed in the same all-white tailored uniforms and helmets and a woman who stepped out of the line a few paces in front of Jacob clicked her heel hard on the floor and bowed her head. She was dressed in the similar tailored military-style uniform but hers was jet black with gold studs on her left shoulder.

"I am Captain Florentina. We will escort you where you need to go, Your Majesty," she said in a thick French accent.

"Thank you, Captain," replied Jacob. Camila lightly touched Jacob's arm to get his attention. "*This could be a trap, Your Majesty,*" said Camila.

"I think it already was a trap. But not for me, for Elliot, and I just hope we're not too late." Genuine concern flowed from Jacob's voice.

"He's smart and talented. Have hope, Your Majesty. And may I apologise for earlier. I addressed you as Your Highness. I wasn't aware of the change in... rank," Camila said slightly embarrassed. Jacob placed his hand on her shoulder and smiled.

"You're always one for proper protocol, Camila. Don't worry. To be honest, I didn't even notice. I am still not used to this yet.

Stay here with my father." Jacob looked at his father and Camila together. *"Camila… if the worst should happen to either myself or Elliot, seeing this through will be yours and my father's responsibility. Yours alone. Do not trust the Royal Council or at least Lady Black until you're sure of their loyalties,"* Jacob continued speaking plainly and clearly to Camila and Johnathan. Camila and Johnathan both gave subtle nods of acknowledgement.

"You're both coming back to me, Jacob," said Johnathan confidently.

Jacob smiled and he and the guards lifted into the air and flew silently and low to the ocean towards Dover Cliff and the entrance of Parliament House.

All Jacob could hear was the whooshing of the wind past his ears and the flapping of his robes as they got closer to the darkened hole in the cliff. Jacob flew a little closer to the Captain Florentina and spoke as quietly as he could over the wind.

"We must be quiet as possible at the entrance. We have no idea what or who is waiting for us," said Jacob. Captain Florentina signalled with her hand that she understood, as they slowed down and approached the entrance.

They set down on a small lip on the edge of the tunnel entrance, Jacob and Captain Florentina at the front and the guards just behind them. A deathly silence filled the dark tunnel as Jacob peered inside the dark abyss and then he looked back around at Florentina.

"This tunnel leads to a large circular building deep within the cliff. That is Parliament House. Underneath that is a secure vault designed to house all the members of Parliament in case of an attack. If Elliot and the members of Parliament are anywhere, it will be there. Follow me," commanded Jacob in a hushed voice. The five of them crept slowly inside the dark tunnel as Jacob noticed one of the guards had lifted his palm with the beginnings of a fire spell but Jacob whipped round closing the guard's palm.

"No! We stay in the dark. There may be MagiWolfs and their masters here," Jacob whispered, as all they could see of each other were their outlines in the dark tunnel. They continued down slowly with Jacob leading the way. Jacob trailed his hand along the stone wall of the tunnel that led for hundreds of feet until finally he felt the walls widen and sensed the space in front of him opening up into a bigger area.

"I think we're here... I think this is Parliament House." Jacobs's whispered words echoed softly around the pitch-black space they found themselves in. Jacob moved cautiously further forward until he tripped and fell onto something soft.

"*Sire!?*" said Captain Florentina.

"*I'm fine. I just tripped on something,*" replied Jacob as he ran his hands over the shape he found himself laying over.

The soft but scratchy warm surface stank of blood and sweat. His hands ran higher as he felt small sticky sharp objects. Jacob breathed in sharply and instantly got back to his feet, his eyes wide, trying to see as much as he could but only the darkness filled his senses.

"It's a dead MagiWolf. They were here," said Jacob quietly, trying to hide the concern in his voice. Jacob knew he had to find the safe room quickly.

"They were here, Your Majesty?" asked Florentina.

"Yes, I think we're too late." Jacob's stomach felt hollow and his mind was only on Elliot. "I think it's time we had some light," he continued as he summoned a fire spell, launching two bright spheres of light into the air. The light instantly filled the giant circular hall they now found themselves in. Huge sharp black marble arched pillars with silver-covered edges caught the fire light that rose up into the domed ceiling. As the fire spheres ascended higher, Jacob could see the hundreds upon hundreds of arched doorways scattered around the walls of the hall that led to different departments of Parliament House but there were signs of a battle throughout the hall. There were charred strikes on the walls from what Jacob guessed were lightning spells. He summoned another fire spell and sent the light towards the centre of the hall. The light revealed the fifty-foot Parliament House Crest which was floating in mid-air. The Queen's golden crown was encircled with a silver disc and engraved in glowing gold writing.

"This Power Given By The People Is To Serve The People"

Jacob, for a moment distracted by the crest, almost didn't notice the figures on the ground in front of him. The fire spheres had begun to light the entire hall and on the dark marble ground lay dozens of the robed lifeless bodies of masters and their MagiWolfs scattered about. Jacob gasped in sharply as he spotted five of the Imperial Guards that Elliot had taken with him also laying lifeless on the ground. Then there was a loud crack that echoed loudly around the hall as Jacob saw something move underneath the floating crest.

"It's the vault door!" said Jacob as out of the ground, a round door opened. He readied himself, summoning a lightning spell to his hands, the electricity bouncing from finger to finger, ready at any moment to strike but then he saw the tip of a Golden Wielding Spear and then the familiar helmet and green robes of an Imperial Guard climbing out of the vault.

"Your Majesty? We thought that was you!" said the guard.

"We?" replied Jacob desperately.

"You'd better come down here, Your Majesty," replied the guard solemnly. The pit in Jacob's stomach grew larger as he closed his eyes briefly and then turned round to Captain Florentina.

"Stay here and guard the vault door," commanded Jacob. Captain Florentina clicked her heel and began issuing commands to her guards. Jacob walked over to the vault door where the Imperial Guard was motioning him down. Jacob peered down to a ladder descending below. The flicker of light came from the bottom of the vault as Jacob then began to climb downwards on the ladder. As he descended and reached the bottom, he could hear the murmuring of voices behind him. He turned around to see most of the Parliamentary Members huddled together in a narrow tunnel with fire spheres summoned along the ceiling. Jacob could see their faces bloodied and full or terror but the first thing he searched for was Elliot. He couldn't see him. The guard had followed him down the ladder and now stood next to Jacob.

"What happened?" Jacob asked the guard quietly.

"We arrived here just as they were opening the vault. Lord Elliot commanded us to round them up and take them back to the Passing Arch and the Imperial City but before we could even start, we were attacked. The MagiWolfs came at us first and then the masters. Lord Elliot rushed as many of them down here as he could but quite a few didn't make it. We managed to fend most of the MagiWolfs off and then the masters suddenly retreated," replied the guard.

"Lord Elliot?" Jacob's voice shook.

"He took a hit but… he's okay, Your Majesty," said the guard, as Jacob let out a shaky long breath of relief.

"Then where is he?" Jacob asked as he looked at the Parliamentary Members.

"After the masters retreated, he didn't want us to bring them out in the open until he knew the Passing Arch was secure," said the guard. Jacob smiled and nodded his head. "He should be back any moment, Your Majesty," continued the guard.

"Very well. Keep them down here for now. I will wait for Lord Elliot up top to make sure the French don't mistake him for someone else when he returns," said Jacob as he began to climb back up the ladder.

Just as Jacob reached the surface, he heard shouting. He looked out towards the tunnel entrance and could see Elliot clutching his side and waving his hands at the French guards.

"LET HIM IN!" shouted Jacob to Captain Florentina. The guards reluctantly submitted to Jacob's command as he clambered out of the vault and to his feet.

"JACOB?" Elliot shouted but his voice was laboured. Jacob ran towards Elliot and threw his arms around him.

"Argh! Ouch," grimaced Elliot. Jacob let go of Elliot instantly and looked him up and down.

"You're hurt?!" said Jacob.

"You're here?" replied Elliot. Jacob laughed and put Elliot's arm around his shoulders and helped him back towards the vault door, setting him down on the ground beside it. Elliot let out a sharp breath as he rested back on the black marble ground. *"You said being in the same place was a bad idea!"* continued Elliot.

"Thomas knew I was coming for my father. So, I assumed he knew about you being here as well," said Jacob as he motioned

towards the dead MagiWolfs and masters scattered on the ground. *"Appears I was correct,"* continued Jacob.

"What happened with Thomas? You fought?" asked Elliot.

"Yes and because of your note to Camila, we came away with our lives," replied Jacob.

"I just thought you might need a little back up… but how did Thomas know you were there though?" asked Elliot.

"I think your mistrust of Lady Black was right. She's the only one that knew where both you and I were going," replied Jacob but Elliot shook his head and looked back at the vault door as Jacob frowned.

"I don't think it was Lady Black that sold us out—" said Elliot as Jacob interrupted him.

"What? You're defending her?" Jacob said stunned.

"I know, it's what I thought too but then I found out that her husband is here. Down there in the vault. He's a Parliamentary Member," Elliot said as he held his side and continued to grimace. Jacob lifted Elliot's robe to one side to get a clearer look at his injury.

"Let me look at that," said Jacob. As he pulled back the robe, he saw a six-inch gash by Elliot's ribs. *"It doesn't look too deep and it's not a MagiWolf bite either. Just need to stop the bleeding,"* Jacob continued as he ripped off a piece of his

sleeve and held it over Elliot's wound. Elliot tensed with the sharp pain.

"So what her husband's here? Maybe she doesn't like him?" said Jacob sarcastically.

"Ha ha, possibly but he's not the only one she has here. Their daughter is here also," revealed Elliot, "so, you see… why would she knowingly tip Thomas off if she knew it would mean the death of her husband and putting her daughter in danger?" continued Elliot.

"That's a fair point. But it also makes everything a little more complicated. If the traitor isn't her then… who?" replied Jacob.

"I don't know." Elliot winced as he moved to stand up and Jacob helped him to his feet. "So, you brought the French here then?" Elliot continued. Jacob nodded and looked at the French guards still standing guard at the tunnel entrance.

"And a fast ship," Jacob said smiling.

"Well, that's handy, because the masters destroyed the Passing Arch and with it, our way out." Elliot motioned back to the vault. "We need to get them out and get them medical attention," continued Elliot. Jacob waved his hand at Captain Florentina who ran over to him at once.

"The people down there. We need to get them out and onto our ship. Can you take care of that while I fly Lord Elliot over?" asked Jacob.

"Of course! At once!" replied Captain Florentina as she commanded her guards to climb down into the vault. Jacob took Elliot firmly and began to walk him back through the long tunnel leading outside.

"Until we know who is tipping Thomas off, we need to keep our circle tight," said Jacob sternly, his words echoing through the tunnel.

"Agreed. So, what's the French ship like then?" asked Elliot as he looked out over the ocean trying to spot it.

"Oh, you'll see!" replied Jacob as he summoned an air spell and lifted them up and out across the ocean towards to French ship.

CHAPTER NINE

VICTORY

❖

Finally, the sun began to rise as Jacob and Elliot set down gently on the French ship's deck. Camila came rushing out of the cabin below as she saw Elliot was clutching his side.

"*He's hurt?*" Camila said, with concern in her voice. Jacob rested Elliot down on the deck floor and looked up at Camila.

"Yes, but it's not too bad, he just needs medical attention to stop the bleeding I think," replied Jacob as King Jean appeared waving his hands at the crewmen, motioning them towards Elliot.

"Get him below deck to the medical bay," commanded King Jean.

"I think there might be more to head that way, Your Majesty," said Jacob as he pointed up in the air behind him where the Parliamentary Members were being escorted with air spells by Captain Florentina and her guards.

The King looked up with his bushy grey eyebrows raised in surprise.

"I see," said the King.

Jacob then looked down to Elliot who was grunting in pain as the medical officers started to lift him onto a stretcher.

"I'll come see you in a moment. Try and rest," said Jacob as he lovingly touched Elliot's shoulder.

"I'll take any excuse for a rest right now!" chuckled Elliot as they carried him below deck.

King Jean shuffled up closer to Jacob, his hand fumbling deep inside his robe pocket and pulling out a piece of MagiChartam. King Jean smiled widely as he handed Jacob the note.

"*Some good news,*" wheezed the King. Jacob opened the note and his eyebrows shot upwards as he looked back up at the King in disbelief.

"*Is this true? Confirmed?*" asked Jacob desperately, his voice filled with hope.

The King nodded slowly, his smile still wide. "*It is! My fleet engaged the American navy and have defeated them swiftly and the remaining ships are in retreat. My army is liberating the outer city and clearing the street of the MagiWolfs and their masters as we speak. Your Empire is saved, Your Majesty,*" King Jean said triumphantly.

Jacob stepped backwards and leant on the deck banister, turning round to look out at the sunrise, feeling its warmth on his face.

"*Thank you for this. We will never forget what you did for us,*" said Jacob, taking both of King Jean's hands in his.

"*Of course. But this King Thomas… he is still alive. He must not be able to escape. He is a threat to all our nations and more importantly, he has followers. He must be killed,*" replied King Jean, narrowing his eyes at Jacob who frowned slightly but nodded in response, pulling his hands away from the King.

"*Captured, yes… but I think there has been enough death for one war. Besides, that would only enrage his followers, plus I don't know what it would mean for my mother if Thomas is* killed," replied Jacob. The King stepped closer to him, his head tilted with intrigue.

"*Explain?*" asked the King.

"My father believes that my mother, during her battle with Thomas, somehow projected her MagiPower around him as she was defeated in order to weaken him. My father also believes he knows a way to return my mother's MagiPower to her but we will need to bring her and Thomas close enough for him to be able to enact the spell. Do you know if Thomas made it back to the Imperial City during the ship's attack?" said Jacob as the King stared out across the horizon.

"There were no reports of his presence. I'd presume he is still on Farland Island recovering from your duel," the King said as he looked back at Jacob, narrowing his eyes again. "*After this spell is enacted… what then?*" continued King Jean.

"Then… if it's successful, my mother and I can defeat Thomas together. When he is at full strength, I cannot fight him alone but with my mother, even if she is weakened, we will have the edge on him but I can't risk fighting him before her MagiPower has been returned. It may kill her if he dies before," replied Jacob.

"Very well… I will help in any way I can to accomplish this," said King Jean as he folded his arms. Jacob nodded once and looked back out towards the rising sun.

"We will have to return to the Imperial City first; my father requires some information from the library and I need to find *out who is passing information to Thomas. My initial suspicions of who it was have been proven wrong. We must keep our plans to ourselves for now. Lady Kerr is the only person that can be trusted outside the Royal Family for now,"* said Jacob as King Jean stepped forward next to him placing his hands on the deck banister joining Jacob looking out at the sun.

"I understand, treachery is hard to root out," said the King.

"If you'll excuse me, Your Majesty, I will check on Lord Elliot," Jacob said as he gave a subtle nod towards the King who reciprocated, nodding back while Jacob made his way below deck towards the medical bay to find Elliot.

CHAPTER TEN

A HOME FALLEN

❖

    The French ship's sparkling sails made haste travelling the length of the English Channel and around the headlands entering Regent's Bay. Jacob stood at the very front of the ship's deck, his robes catching the wind behind him and the air brushing his dark hair. His eyes began to glass over as the image of the grand and imposing statues of past Kings and Queens, that once rose majestically out of the ocean that created a lane for ships to sail into to the city harbour, had now all but crumbled and cracked from the fierce battles back into the ocean below. Jacob felt a presence behind him and as he looked round, he saw Elliot and Camila were also looking at the destruction of their home. Jacob looked at Elliot and then pointed to his injured side.

"How's the cut?" asked Jacob.

"Patched up good. They have impressive healers onboard," replied Elliot as he motioned his head towards the Imperial City and the Royal Palace at its centre. *"At least the fires are out,"* continued Elliot as the three of them could now see the outer city sandstone-coloured buildings that only a few days ago were a blaze with flames now just emitting a dark grey smoke out of the fallen walls. As they drew closer, the level of destruction of the outer city become clearer. Jacob let his mouth open slightly as he wished his eyes were deceiving him. The southern wall had been completely destroyed; the huge stone bricks twice as big as the ship they were on had fallen onto the cliffs below and broken into smaller pieces scattered along the shoreline. Most of the buildings around the outer city had completely crumbled down onto the streets and the ones that remained had only a wall or two left. The closer the ship got, the deeper into the inner city and the Royal Palace they could see; they were still being protected by the new barrier spell and thus the destruction within it was less heartbreaking.

Elliot and Camila walked up either side of Jacob, taking his hands in theirs.

"Buildings can be rebuilt my son." Johnathan had silently walked up to stand beside Elliot, leaning forward slightly to look at Jacob whose eyes were still fixed on the city.

"And the lives lost?" said Jacob, his voice full of sorrow and anger.

"We make sure the ones who lived remember them forever," Johnathan replied. As Jacob turned his head to look at him, a single tear fell from Jacob's eye. "*I am very pleased for you two, Elliot. I am proud to call you my son-in-law,*" continued Johnathan as he placed his hand on Elliot's shoulder.

"PREPARE TO DOCK!" shouted the helmsman from behind them. The ship's sails began to be hoisted in as they approached the city harbour. Jacob could see four other bronze-coloured French warships had already docked, their white-uniformed soldiers coming and going along the harbour gangplanks, some carrying stretchers with their wounded. As they passed through the giant arched harbour defence gates, which had also seen their fair share of cannon fire, King Jean had walked up to join the four of them.

Jacob took a step back and turned to them. "*I need to inform you of some decisions I have made. In light of the situation we are faced with, not knowing who the traitor is passing information to Thomas, we have to assume he or she is a member of the Royal Council. Until we capture Thomas, I don't see how we'll find out. So... until that time... the Royal Council's authority must be suspended.*" Jacob spoke confidently and with pure authority as Camila and Johnathan looked at each other in surprise while Elliot nodded in agreement.

"While I agree with the decision, they will object, Your Majesty," said Camila sternly as Jacob shrugged his shoulders.

"Which is why I am appointing you as City Regent to oversee things while the Queen, my father, Elliot and myself are gone. Hopefully that will quell some of the objections from the Royal Council," replied Jacob.

Johnathan then stepped forward and motioned his hand towards the Parliamentary Members who were now appearing on the ship's deck getting ready to disembark, their robes and faces still dirtied and blood stained.

"What about them? Only three quarters remain alive after the attack at Parliament House," asked Johnathan. Jacob turned around and looked down at them.

"Their roll is more important now than ever. They were elected by the people and their voices must be heard but, until Thomas is captured, we are the leadership of the British Empire of Magic," replied Jacob, turning back around and looking at Camila, Elliot and Johnathan, "and with the help of our allies, like my father said, we will rebuild," continued Jacob, as King Jean nodded at Jacob. The ship rocked to one side as it docked in the harbour, the crewmen throwing ropes overboard to secure the ship as the gangplanks were lowered.

"So, the plan to capture Thomas?" asked Elliot.

"First, I must call the Royal Council for an emergency meeting. Camila, if you could see to that. And I'll inform them of their suspension," said Jacob. Camila nodded sharply and then stepped forward raising her hands shoulder-height palm-up to summon an air spell. The air spun around her as she was lifted with speed into the air and darted sharply towards the Royal Palace.

"Father, I need you to do whatever you need to do at the library to prepare for the spell to return mother's MagiPower to her. Elliot, I need you to have the Queen brought here to this ship as quietly as possible. No one must know she is being moved," continued Jacob.

"Okay," replied Elliot.

"It won't take me long," Johnathan stated as he quickly summoned his air spell and lifted speedily into the air behind Camila. Jacob watched his father fly into the distance and then lifted his dark hood over his head while looking at Elliot.

"Once all this is done, we will head straight for the White Islands. King Jean and I believe Thomas is still there recovering on Farland Island. I hope this is acceptable to you King Jean?" Jacob said, now looking straight at King Jean.

"But of course, my fleet and army can remain here to keep the city secure," replied King Jean.

"Very generous of you, Your Majesty, especially as our navy is all but sunk and the Imperial Guard a quarter of its original size. We will need all the help we can get to keep order in the city. I'll have Harriet the Caretaker taken to her son, Lennard.

She has been through enough—" King Jean raised his hand gently to interrupt Jacob.

"*Forgive me, Your Majesty, but is it wise to have the only two people in your Empire capable of operating the Passing Dome in the same place?*" asked King Jean as Jacob frowned slightly.

"*As opposed to anywhere else? The Palace is the safest place for them at the moment,*" Jacob replied brushing off King Jean's comments. "*As for Kendra and her son, we must keep them hidden within the Higher Palace for now. Elliot, take them with you now, speak to Camila and make arrangements for their safety and then return with mother,*" continued Jacob.

Elliot nodded confidently and strode off below deck to find Kendra and her son. Jacob made his way to the centre of the upper forward deck between the huge masts holding the hoisted sails and began to summon his air spell. He looked over at King Jean briefly who was still stood at the very front of the ship, his hand resting on the banister to steady his frail body.

"*If you wish to stay at the Palace while we take care of Thomas I will understand, Your Majesty,*" offered Jacob as the end from his air spell whooshed around him. King Jean stood up straight and looked deep into Jacob's eyes.

"*Oh, I wouldn't miss this fight for anything,*" King Jean said defiantly. Jacob nodded and smiled.

"*Very well. I will return shortly,*" said Jacob as he shot into the air at great speed.

CHAPTER ELEVEN

THE ROYAL COUNCIL

❖

Jacob landed softly within the courtyard in front of the Lower Palace entrance. He looked around at the charred grass and burnt trees of the courtyard gardens. Although it was merely days ago he was there with Camila and Elliot, rushing to the Passing Dome to bring the Imperial Guard through from Colghorn, it felt like a lifetime ago. He noticed the French soldiers patrolling in pairs through the gardens in their white uniforms doing as King Jean said they would, keeping the city secure and while Jacob was pleased to see them, an intense sadness and guilt fell over him. The countless lives of his own people weighed deeply. He tried to shake off the emotion and carried on walking towards the Palace entrance where two Imperial Guards stood side by side, their golden wielding spears crossed, blocking the gigantic stone doors. As he walked up to them, he lowered his hood, revealing his face as he looked up at them. The guards looked at each other in surprise and shock and uncrossed their spears immediately.

"Your Majesty! We didn't see it was you. Our apologies," said the guard to Jacob's left. The other guard placed his hand on the stone doors and, in an instant, they opened up with a loud crack, the creaking echoing within the huge circular hall inside. Jacob lowered his head, subtly acknowledging the guards, and began to walk inside.

"Do you require an escort, Your Majesty?" asked the guard

"Not necessary," Jacob replied, raising his hand subtly as he continued through the King's Hall. He looked up at the enormous statue of the First King made of pure gold. He smiled to himself briefly and began to climb the large sand-coloured stone staircase leading to the Higher Palace. Atop the curving staircase he walked the long hallway leading to the Royal Council Chamber with fire spheres lighting the way. As he passed his own apartment entrance, he hesitated for a moment as a mixture of memories and emotions filed his mind before he continued on.

He stood at the threshold of the large arched stone doors of the Royal Council Chamber. He breathed in deeply and centred himself. He raised his hand and summoned a small pushing spell that forced the large stone doors to open slowly. As the doors opened, Jacob could see the eleven Royal Council members standing around the High Table including Camila who was stood at the far end of the dark stone table. Jacob looked at her and nodded.

"My fellow council members, if you'd take your seats, King Jacob wishes to address you," said Camila loudly.

The council members, one by one, took their seats and then looked up at Jacob in anxious anticipation. He walked up and stood by his mother's throne seat at the head of the High Table. He looked down at it as his mind drifted for a fleeting moment to his mother and then looked back at the council members, briefly resting his eyes on Lady Black, her dark eyes narrowed sharply on Jacob.

"I'll remain standing if you don't mind? It doesn't feel quite right to sit in her chair just now," said Jacob softly as he rested his right hand on the top of the throne chair, holding it tight.

"As you all know, our Empire is going through the most unstable and challenging time since the MagiWars over five hundred years ago. We've faced our biggest enemy and suffered great losses but with the help of our allies, the French Kingdom of Magic, King Jean's navy and his army has helped us take back this city from the enemy. That said… the so-called King Thomas of the Dark Knights is still at large and our Empire will not be safe until he is captured. Myself, Prince Johnathan, Lady Kerr and Lord Elliot have a plan to do just this," continued Jacob as the council members looked at each other subtly.

"Most of you will be aware by now that Lord Elliot left to bring the Parliamentary Members back here to the Palace from Dover Cliff for their protection. I also attempted a prisoner exchange to bring my father, Prince Johnathan, home. Both of these missions were successful in part. But we suffered losses, unnecessary losses, due to what we now understand as a traitor among us at the highest level, passing information to the *enemy."* Murmuring around the High Table was intensifying as Jacob continued.

"With that in mind, it has left me little choice but to limit the authority over the Empire to the Royal Family and place Royal Lady Kerr as interim City Regent."

"How dare you!" shouted Lady Black as she stood up from chair in protest. *"You think one of us a traitor?"* continued Lady Black in protest as Jacob raised his hands calmly in response.

"Please, Lady Black. At this moment in time, I do not know who or indeed if any of this council are responsible for these information leaks, which is why, until we have uncovered the traitor, the leadership circle must be tightened. We are so close to ending this that we cannot afford any more mistakes. Lady Kerr will liaise with the members of Parliament who represent the villages and towns within the Empire and ensure the MagiWolf and masters' threat is abating… I did not come to this decision lightly. As you know, my mother stood for a new democracy within our Empire and that is engrained in me and so it shall return. Your objection will be noted but for now, as your King, it is within my power to do this and… my word is final." Jacob looked squarely at Lady Black, his face showing no signs of expression but his hand gripped the throne chair so tightly his nails dug into the stone surface.

Lady Black, who was still standing up out of her chair, looked around the room as the rest of the council members began to lower their heads and nodded submissively towards King Jacob.

"*This is unprecedented!*" barked Lady Black at Jacob.

"*Perhaps so, Lady Black. But you aren't exactly unfamiliar with breaks of procedure yourself, are you? For instance, your marriage to a member of Parliament has been concealed from this council and indeed your Queen for the sole reason it's a conflict of interests and forbidden. Both your husband and daughter are safe and well thanks to the efforts of Lord Elliot and his guard, I might add,*" Jacob said, his eyes narrowed directly into hers. She briefly cast her gaze across the council members and Lady Kerr, who had the faintest of smiles appearing in the corner of her mouth as she brushed her blonde hair to one side. Lady Black slowly lowered herself back into her chair and looked down at the High Table submissively. Jacob nodded confidently and looked back at the rest of the council.

"*Very well. It is done. Remember this is temporary. For now, I must leave you in the capable command of Lady Kerr,*" said Jacob as Lady Kerr rose out of her chair and bowed her head towards Jacob who smiled and bowed back before turning around and walking out of the Royal Council Chamber, summoning a pushing spell to close the doors behind him. As the stone door slammed shut, Jacob dropped his head down and let out a deep and long sigh, rubbing his face in his hands. Jacob then began to make his way back along the hallway towards the stairs to the King's Hall but he heard the doors of the council chamber crack open behind him making him stop and turn his head, looking back to see Camila walking hastily towards him as Jacob turned around to face her.

"*I wanted to catch you before you left,*" said Camila as she placed her hand on his arm. "*I've spoken with the members of Parliament that survived Dover Cliff. As you know, each of the members represent the people of the regions or towns of our Empire. From what they have told me, there is great unrest, a divide for want of a better word.*" Camila looked at Jacob with genuine concern in her eyes. "*This war with King Thomas, forgive me for saying, and this is a delicate matter, but it seems to have raised doubt in your leadership and the Queen's amongst the MagiFolk. The Parliamentary Members are telling me there is a growing number of our people that agree with King Thomas and his vision for our future,*" continued Camila.

"*I see. It would appear that Thomas is getting his way even with a defeated army and navy. Thank you, Camila… this is indeed important information. While I am away do what you can to keep Parliament on our side. The last thing we need right now is a civil war,*" replied Jacob as his voice echoed gently off the stone walls.

"*I will do everything I can… Please be careful out there. I know your mother said it already but, put all your trust in Lord Elliot. He will never betray you,*" continued Camila. They hugged tightly as he felt their bond of friendship was stronger than ever.

"*Talking of Lord Elliot, he has taken your mother to the ship and awaits you there with your father. I believe he has what he needs from the library,*" Camila said as she leant back from their embrace.

"Kendra and the baby?" Jacob asked.

"I've put them in the rooms opposite your mother's private apartment. No one dares go near that part of the Palace as they believe her still in residence, so it should be sufficient in keeping them out of sight for now," replied Camila as she motioned down the hallway.

"Good, I will pay them a quick visit before I leave. Thank you, Camila… you're going to have your hands full here!" chuckled Jacob as Camila shrugged and looked back towards the council chamber.

"I can handle them. It's what I do," Camila said comically.

Jacob put his hand on her shoulder, smiled and turned around and carried on down the hallway past the staircase leading to the King's Hall. At the end of the hallway a small stone bridge covered in creeping ivy connected the Higher Palace to the Queen's residence and rooms where Kendra and her baby were. As Jacob walked over the bridge, he could see the entire city and harbour where the French ships were docked. The city still looked majestic even through the destruction, fire-scarred buildings and lands. A sense of pride washed over Jacob as he looked out. He continued onto another sand-coloured stone hallway with the familiar stone doors that led to his mother's apartment sealed shut. Jacob knocked lightly on the doors opposite. Kendra's soft footsteps approached the door.

"Who is it?" asked Kendra.

"It's Jacob."

The door opened a few inches as Kendra peered through the gap at Jacob warily.

"It's just me," said Jacob. Kendra opened the door wide and motioned for Jacob to enter.

Jacob entered the lavishly furnished room with a white oak dining table by a large stone patio overlooking the city. Kendra was dressed in a cream satin night gown, her thick dark blonde hair resting neatly on her shoulders. She walked over to a large white oak four poster bed where her baby lay cooing. Jacob followed her and leant forward, looking at the baby lovingly.

"You're going to fight him again, aren't you?" Kendra said, her eyes locked on her baby, "Thomas, I mean."

"I have to try and find a way to end all this hate and war, Kendra. You'll both be safe here under Lady Kerr's protection while I am away. You can trust her," said Jacob as he leant back to look at Kendra. She looked at him, nodding softly.

"If you fail and Thomas finds out about him," Kendra said motioning her hand towards the baby, "he will kill anyone to find him, including me and Neville, especially him. I need you to promise me you will take care of my son no matter what happens... promise me, Jacob? Protect him from Thomas," pleaded Kendra.

"*You have my word, Kendra,*" replied Jacob, taking Kendra's hand in his.

"*I will give my life for my son, Jacob. His life is here now,*" said Kendra as she looked out of the patio window at the city. "*You have given him a chance at a good life and you have my loyalty for that… for what it's worth,*" continued Kendra as she locked eyes with Jacob.

"*Loyalty seems to be a finite commodity these days… Thank you, Kendra. Welcome to the family,*" Jacob said as he pointed to a painting of his mother on the wall by the patio window, "*and we are naming that baby when I return!*" Jacob chuckled over his shoulder as he walked over to the patio doors summoning an air spell. In an instant he was pulled into the air above, leaving the patio curtains flapping violently from his air spell.

CHAPTER TWELVE

THE FINAL PLAN

❖

Jacob circled above the Higher Place, smiling as he saw the Royal Gardens and the memories he had made there with his family and Elliot. Thankfully the new barrier spell had protected most of the palace from the destruction the rest of the outer city endured over the last few days of conflict. As he veered off towards the harbour, he could see more of the French soldiers in the streets below, some of them patrolling with what was left of the Imperial Guard. The sense of relief that the city and palace were secure thanks to King Jean was the only thing keeping his stomach from lurching more with the nerves of what he knew was coming.

He flew with haste, diving down over the sharp cliffs and into the harbour. He noticed that King Jean's ship was now the only French warship left in the harbour and as he looked out across the island coastline, he could see the entire French fleet had now created a protection blockade around the city. Jacob touched down on the ship's deck softly, where he noticed all the crewmen rushing from mast to mast opening the sparkling and transparent sails preparing the ship to leave. King Jean appeared through the commotion of crewmen wearing a long white robe with polished black amour underneath covering his entire body. Jacob noticed he was walking with ease compared to before. As King Jean approached Jacob, he wrapped his knuckles on his chest amour and smiled.

"Ah yes, another marvel made by our constructors! Not only does this armour protect me from most spells, it makes me feel like I'm a teenager again!" said King Jean.

Jacob gave the impression he was suitably impressed by the boastful King by nodding his head and raising his eyebrows. *"Your father and Lord Elliot await us below deck with your mother. Please follow me,"* King Jean continued as he turned on his heel and strode off across the bronze decks and in through the cabin hatch that led to the decks below.

As Jacob entered through the hatch, he followed King Jean down a spiralling ramp descending downward, in the same bronze material that covered the rest of the ship. As they reached the bottom of the ramp, two of the French soldiers stood guard next to a lone hatch door. As soon as they saw King Jean and Jacob, they touched the hatch door and it clunked open immediately.

As the hatch opened, Jacob instantly saw his mother in the middle of the large cabin in a medical bay bed still unconscious, just as he had left her. Elliot and Johnathan stood over the Queen on either side, both of them intensely studying and flipping the pages of books so much they hadn't noticed Jacob or King Jean enter.

"I had the entire medical bay converted to a recovery space for your mother and to prepare for the spell," said King Jean, making Elliot and Johnathan look up.

"I'm constantly impressed by how quickly you and your people get things done, Your Majesty," replied Jacob as Johnathan began to wave his book in the air at Jacob.

"Good, you're here. I think we've figured it out," said Johnathan, motioning his head at Elliot. Jacob walked up next to Elliot looking down at his mother who looked peaceful and if you didn't know better was having the most pleasant of naps.

"Explain, please?" asked Jacob, looking at his father.

"Firstly, your mother has most definitely used a MagiPower Projection spell to hinder King Thomas's abilities. So, we were right about that... I believe I have found a way of pulling her back without making the same mistake Otyre made all those years ago. He left his own body to pull her back because he didn't know another way. I do... The projection spell your mother has used creates a kind of tether between her body and her MagiPower. It can only project one way at a time, which is why Otyre never came back; he used his own link to send her back but it left him disconnected. The spell that Elliot and I have created can reverse her projection, forcing her MagiPower back into her body without us leaving ours," said Johnathan who was nodding frantically. *"We can do this!"* he continued, not hiding the excitement from his voice.

"Good work! How close will mother and Thomas need to be for this to work?" asked Jacob.

"Within line of sight," replied Johnathan with a slight shrug of his shoulders.

"Hold on, that's not definite. This is guess work," interjected Elliot.

"Elliot's right. This has never been done before; there are unknowns for all of it," admitted Johnathan.

"Do you at least know the risks to her?" Jacob said, motioning his hand towards his mother.

"The one thing we know for sure is if King Thomas dies or even if he is weakened too much before we have returned the MagiPower to your mother, she will be lost forever. She is linked to his own MagiPower, meaning if he is weakened, she will feel it twice as much... Technically speaking, she should've been lost to us when you fought Thomas the last time. There is no way her MagiPower can endure anything like that again," Johnathan said sternly.

"Then we best keep him busy!" King Jean said as he walked up beside Johnathan. They all looked at Jacob knowingly.

"Yes, I am aware that is my job. King Jean, can your people keep this ship hidden with masking spells for long enough while I divert Thomas and my father and Elliot perform the spell?" Jacob asked, looking at King Jean, who nodded once with confidence.

"Of course, the Queen's safety is of my utmost concern," wheezed King Jean, "you have my word on that." King Jean placed his hand comfortingly on Johnathan's shoulder.

"Good. Once this spell is complete, Thomas will surely know what's happened. He will be at full power, unhindered and outranged. It's going to take all of us to bring him down. Do you think mother will be strong enough to fight, father?" said Jacob.

"I can't say for certain, but there's a good chance. Besides, knowing your mother, as soon as she finds out what's going on, you won't be able to stop her getting back into the fight," replied Johnathan.

"Or me!" exclaimed Elliot looking straight into Jacob's eyes.

"Normally I would protest to the motion that all of us should be out there in harm's way, for the pure reason of succession, but these are most definitely not normal times or a normal enemy. We all need to be out there against him," Jacob said, returning Elliot's stare, "except for you, Your Majesty, I don't expect you to put you or your Kingdom's future at stake in this way," Jacob continued, now looking at King Jean.

"Ha! It's true I am an old man but there is a little left in me yet. I will do my part in the fight. As far as we know, all of King Thomas's forces, the MagiWolfs, masters and the American fleet, were all at the Imperial City, so we can only expect a handful of *guards loyal to the White Islands. I am sure my soldiers and I can take care of them,"* chuckled King Jean.

"Very well. Once Thomas is defeated, he is to be captured, alive—" commanded Jacob as Johnathan interrupted.

"I had a thought about that. The last few years, the spell makers and I have been experimenting on linking spells with magical ley lines... and the ley lines on Farland Island are amongst the most powerful in the world. I can link a binding spell to them and not even Thomas would be powerful enough to break it. Of course, he will have to be severely weakened to place the said binding spell on him and he will have to remain on Farland for the spell to continue to be effective."

Jacob raised his eyebrows and nodded as King Jean turned to face Johnathan closely.

"Perhaps you can show me how this is done? After all, it would be unwise for only one of us to know how such a spell is performed in the heat of battle? Also, selfishly, I might add, this would be very valuable to my constructors," said King Jean.

Jacob smiled and nodded at his father. *"Surely it's the least we can do to thank you, Your Majesty,"* said Jacob, his father nodding his head in agreement.

"Excellent. I will give the order to get us underway to the White Islands immediately," King Jean said as he made haste out of the medical bay and back up the spiral ramp leading to the upper deck.

Jacob watched King Jean leave and then looked back at Johnathan and Elliot. *"We end this today,"* said Jacob. Elliot and Johnathan looked at each other briefly.

"When she comes around, that'll mean she'll be Queen again and she might not be happy about all this," said Johnathan, looking down at his wife and then back up, eyeing Jacob.

"I know what you're implying, father. She will have wanted me to sacrifice her so I can kill Thomas while he is weakened. I will gladly face her judgment if it means putting a stop to all of this," Jacob said decisively.

CHAPTER THIRTEEN

KING THOMAS

❖

Minutes felt like hours and hours felt like days for Jacob as he waited at his mother's side to arrive at Farland Island. He looked down upon his mother's expressionless face laying there in the plain-sheeted medical bed; he wondered what he would have done in her place all those years ago when she made the decision to hide the truth of his grandfather's crimes against Thomas's parents. In just the short time he had been King, he began to empathise more than ever that hard choices have to be made for the future and protection of the people and Empire. He judged her so much for what she had done but now he felt himself thinking he may have done the same thing if it were him faced with that choice. The faint sounds of footsteps came from behind, breaking his train of thought. He turned his head to see Elliot, who was now dressed in his dark green Imperial robes with a smooth plating of silver amour down his right arm.

"We're here," said Elliot plainly. Jacob stood up from his chair at his mother side, straightening his glistening silver-plated amour which was wrapped around his chest and neck.

"The masking spells?" asked Jacob.

"They seem to be doing the trick. There's no movement on Farland to suggest they know we are here," replied Elliot.

"Very well. We need to move her to the upper deck for this to work, don't we?" Jacob said, motioning his hand towards his mother. Elliot nodded softly while he looked at the Queen for a moment.

"I've got people coming down now to move her up," replied Elliot as Jacob walked over towards the spiral ramp.

"Good, let's go then," said Jacob and both of them climbed the ramp back outside to the upper deck, passing Johnathan and half a dozen medical crew making their way down to the Queen.

As they emerged outside, Jacob could see the French soldiers lined up in four perfect squares facing Captain Florentina. King Jean was standing at the front of the ship, staring out at the rugged coastline of Farland Island. Jacob turned to Elliot and looked directly into his bright blue eyes.

"How long will you and my father need to complete the spell to return the MagiPower back to mother?" asked Jacob.

"Once we start... ten or so minutes. It's hard to say for sure. But you'll know when it's done. You'll sense Thomas's power return to full strength... Talking of which, what's your plan to keep him busy while your father and I do this?" said Elliot.

"I've got an idea or two. Thomas always liked to talk so I'm counting on that as I can't fight him until you two have done your job. As soon as mother is awake, I am going to need you all by my side to fight him," replied Jacob. Elliot smiled and rocked his head back, his eyebrows raised.

"Trust me, nothing is going to keep me away from this fight. It's going to be the battle of century! They'll write songs about it one day and I want my name in there!" laughed Elliot.

"Well, I am glad your ego is on our side!" chuckled Jacob.

"Excuse me, Your Majesty," said a crewman behind Jacob and Elliot. The two of them turned around and moved out of the way as the Queen was being carried on a long stretcher to the middle of the outside deck followed by Prince Johnathan eyeing their every move.

"*Please be careful with her!*" said Johnathan emotionally.

They placed her down gently in the middle of the white-uniformed soldiers. Jacob put his hood over his head and walked over to his father with Elliot following.

"*Right, this bit is up to you. I will keep Thomas talking for as long as I can for you to perform the spell,*" said Jacob.

Johnathan and Elliot both nodded confidently. Jacob left them standing over the Queen and made his way up the bronze-coloured steps to the front of the ship, next to King Jean who turned his head towards Jacob.

"*It's time, young King,*" said King Jean.

"*Indeed, it is. You and your soldiers will keep the Farland guards busy?*" replied Jacob.

"*Of course, you have my word. We stand with you to defeat King Thomas,*" said King Jean as the two of them looked at each other intensely for a moment until Jacob nodded and looked out at the crashing waves upon the cliffs of Farland Island.

"*Watch out for Neville, the Lady Regent's son-in-law. What he lacks in imagination he makes up for in raw magical talent,*" said Jacob.

King Jean tilted his head slightly and smiled back. Jacob stepped a few feet forward, closed his eyes, took a deep breath and centred his mind.

He raised his hands level with his chest and summoned an air spell, which lifted him quickly into the air above. He rose higher and higher until he was free of the masking spell about a hundred feet above the ship. Now all Jacob could hear was the sounds of the wind whooshing past his ears and the faint smell of salt air and seaweed. He could see the Regent's Hall and the damage done by the cannon fire days ago. As he hung there in the air, there was a moment of serenity; he hadn't been spotted yet and the world seemed calm.

He brought his hands together and focused his mind and magic on the ocean below him. He summoned the water upwards towards him like a giant waterfall in reverse. As the water approached his feet, he threw his hands out wide, casting the water in a circular motion, forming a table-like surface beneath him. Jacob now brought his hands together above his head, summoning the air around him with such force the clouds above began to swirl within the spell. In an instant he threw his hands downward towards the lapping rapids of the water beneath him. As the air spell struck the surface of the water, it began to freeze at such a speed that within seconds, the water rising from the ocean froze solid into a smooth table-like surface. Jacob floated down to the surface of the hundred-foot ice island he had now created above the ship. He then brought both his hands to his side and summoned a powerful fire spell, then throwing the fire ball flying towards the Regent's Hall; clapping his hands together, the fire ball exploded thirty feet about the hall.

"That should get his attention," Jacob said aloud to himself.

In the distance he saw a dark figure shoot upwards into the sky above the Regent's Hall and hang there suspended in the air for a moment. He knew straightaway that it was Thomas. Jacob's stomach lurched slightly for a second but he controlled his nerves with a deep breath as Thomas began to fly straight towards him. Within seconds, Thomas was ten feet in front of Jacob floating gently down landing on the frozen surface. His hood also placed over his head, Jacob saw his green eyes staring straight into his. He knew that Elliot and his father would have spotted Thomas already and started casting the spell to bring his mother back.

"Hello, old friend," said Jacob.

"Friend? It's interesting you think we are still friends," snarled Thomas.

"You and I have shared a lot of tragedy and betrayal, Thomas. You were right, the truth of my grandfather's crimes must be known to the world and my mother was complicit in hiding that truth. Come with me, answer for your actions and I swear to you, I will deliver justice for your parents' murder," said Jacob.

Thomas stepped a few feet closer to Jacob, lowering his hood but not breaking his eye contact with Jacob.

"So small-minded, Jacob. You're still that boy that is just happy with his lot in life and thinks the world is sparkly bright, aren't you?" Thomas shook his head and looked back at Farland Island. *"You see that Island? It's where all this started.*

Do you know how easy it was to convince the Lady Regent that she should ally with me? It was easy because your family's arrogance in your right to rule this Empire has sullied not just their pride in being MagiFolk but all of your so-called subjects. Meanwhile all of our kind are being starved of our rightful freedom over this world by the equally arrogant humans. It's not about getting justice, as you call it, for my parents, Jacob... it's about why they were murdered. Their name... tell me Jacob, does that make you and your family fit to rule?" Thomas continued looking back at Jacob.

"I will not be judged for my family's crimes, Thomas. You're so blinded by hate and your own entitlement you can't see what you've done to our kind by starting all this off. You've created a division that could lead us to a civil war no matter who wins this fight between us. You tell me, Thomas... does that make you fit to rule?" said Jacob, narrowing his eyes at Thomas and clenching his fists. "No, besides, this is over. You've lost your forces. We've sunk the navy of the American Republic of Magic and you failed to kill the Queen or the Royal Council. I'm standing before you today, as a friend, offering you a chance to keep your life. Surrender peacefully and your sentence will not be death," said Jacob.

"You have your mother's arrogance, Jacob. Surrender? Why would I do that? You said it yourself, our people are on the verge of a civil war... Tell me, how many do you think will fight for you and how many will fight for m——" Thomas stopped mid-sentence and stumbled backwards very slightly. Jacob knew immediately what was happening. His mother's MagiPower was returning to her and leaving Thomas.

"Wha—? What is happening? It's your mother! She is why I have been weakened!" bellowed Thomas as he fell onto one knee, placing his left hand down on the icy surface to steady himself, his other hand summoning a fire spell, the flames licking his palm and fingers.

He looked up at Jacob, his eyes full of anger and then, turning his head sideways, he looked confused for a moment but he pushed himself back up to his feet. He threw his arms out wide with a bolt of lightning striking his left hand, absorbing its power. Jacob took a few steps back and summoned a barrier spell with as much power as he could muster just before Thomas sent both the fire and lightning spell hurtling towards Jacob with a piercing crack and rumble as the spells hit his barrier. The pure force of Thomas's spells penetrated through the barrier, emitting a shockwave towards Jacob, sending him spinning backwards, striking the icy surface hard, winding him badly.

Jacob's head was ringing as he tried to desperately focus his eyes back on Thomas. Wiping the blood from his mouth, he clambered to his feet as he clutched his chest, trying to force the air back into his lungs. Thomas was walking forward towards Jacob with bolts of electricity bouncing from hand to hand as if he was playing with it. An evil smile fell across his face and Jacob knew he had his full power returned to him. Behind Thomas three more figures appeared flying towards them. Jacob stood up straight and summoned his own lightning spell to his hands, the electricity wrapping along his fingers.

"*All alone, Jacob?*" snarled Thomas as Lady Regent Catherine, Neville and Kiron landed next to him.

Jacob looked around him, his heart thumping hard in his chest, flooding his ears with the sound of his rushing heartbeat. He closed his eyes and put his trust in his family, allies and his husband. The ice beneath his feet began to shake and as he opened his eyes, he knew what it was... he felt what he'd been longing to feel for days – his mother's presence.

"*My son has never been alone, Thomas.*" The Queen appeared, floating majestically in the air behind Jacob, her white robes flapping in the wind, the air flowing through her thick dark hair and brown eyes narrowing on Thomas.

Elliot, Johnathan and King Jean rose up either side of the Queen as Jacob looked around to see them. The Queen motioned them forward onto the icy surface next to Jacob with a tilt of her head. They floated forward and landed next to him as he turned back around to face Thomas whose focus had changed, solely on the Queen.

"*This ends now, Thomas. Surender,*" ordered the Queen.

"*Not now and never to you!*" barked Thomas as he threw his hands forward, sending out multiple bolts of lightning at them.

Jacob, Elliot and Johnathan all summoned barrier spells in front of them. Another piercing crack filled the air as the lightning met the barrier spell but this time rendering

Thomas's lightning useless. The Queen behind Jacob rose her hands above her head pulling the ocean beneath to rise up and spiral around her at great speed and then, in an instant, the water stopped moving and froze into tiny sharp arrows pointed at Thomas. With a graceful wave of the back of her hand, she sent hundreds of the frozen arrows speeding at Thomas who summoned the ice surface he was standing on upwards, forming it into a wall blocking the arrows from striking him and those behind.

Thomas looked around at Lady Regent Catherine. *"SUMMON YOUR GUARDS HERE!"* he shouted.

The Lady Regent hesitantly brushed her fingers over a smooth golden bracelet on her wrist which glowed bright white, summoning her guards to her. Within a few moments, ten of the Farland Island guards came flying towards them. Queen Ellaryne floated forward and gently set down on the icy surface next to Jacob, Elliot and Johnathan, her white robes trailing behind her. She looked over at King Jean who was standing just to one side of them and nodded her head at him. He clapped his hands above his head and seconds later, Captain Florentina and twenty of her soldiers appeared from below, landing next to King Jean.

Thomas clicked his fingers and the icy wall he summoned shattered. The ten Farland guards had now also landed next to Lady Regent Catherine with Neville and Kiron standing ready next to Thomas. The Queen now stepped forward in front of Jacob, looking at him with a warm smile and a subtle brush of her hand on his arm. They both nodded at each other and Jacob knew this was the moment they had to all pull together to defeat Thomas.

"This is your last chance, Thomas," said the Queen.

Thomas looked around at Kiron and Neville and nodded his head sharply. He then focused his green eyes on his hands in front of him summoning a ball of electricity between them.

Kiron and Neville followed his cue and summoned the same spell into their hands. The Queen slowly raised her hands skyward, commanding the clouds above to gather with lightning and thunder rumbling. Jacob, Elliot and Johnathan all raised their hands together, feeling the power above, while Lady Regent Catherine commanded her guards to attack with fire spells being thrown back and forth between the French and Farland guards; even King Jean himself was launching multiple powerful fire spells from both his hands at them.

Thomas, Neville and Kiron emitted their blindingly bright spell towards the Queen but she, Jacob, Elliot and Johnathan had already harnessed the power of the lightning above and all four of them projected the bolts at Thomas, their spells meeting with the loudest sound of cracking and rumbling that would've been heard for miles around. Stray bolts of lightning and electricity surges exploded from the meeting of the spells, striking and splitting the icy surface they were standing on. Chunks of ice fell the hundred feet back into the ocean below as all seven of the sorcerers were flooding their MagiPower into the spell, but Jacob could sense that they were gaining ground on Thomas as Neville and Kiron were weakening quickly.

He took advantage of the opportunity and focused his mind with every ounce of concentration he could gather and summoned a second spell, this time a water spell in unison with the lightning. His water spell manipulated the icy surface into razor sharp spears that shot out from the ground beneath and into the shoulders of Neville and Kiron. They both instantly broke off their spell with Thomas and clutched their pierced shoulders, blood dripping onto the ice as they fell to the ground in pain.

With Neville and Kiron defeated, it was enough for the Queen, Jacob, Elliot and Johnathan to start to overpower Thomas. The centre of their spell was moving closer and closer towards Thomas, his face and bright green eyes contorted in an effort to hold them back in vain. In one last ditch attempt, Thomas allowed their spell to engulf him as he created a barrier spell around his body, the lightning striking with loud claps and cracks. He summoned the most powerful fire spell Jacob had ever seen into the air above them. The huge giant ball of fire swirled, growing ever bigger and bigger until it sent a line of molten hot fire at them. Instantly, the Queen, Jacob, Elliot and Johnathan summoned a powerful barrier spell and the fire struck and rippled along the barrier until the Queen managed to control the flames upwards and redirected it with even more force than Thomas's own spell retaliating it back towards him.

Thomas's face showed a brief moment of surprise and shock before he placed his hands on his own barrier spell in an attempt to reinforce it. The Queen's fire spell struck it and the renewed force of her spell pushed Thomas backwards, stumbling to his knees. The flames relentlessly pounded his barrier spell while Jacob, Elliot and Johnathan continued their attack with the lightning spells. Jacob could see Thomas was weakened and his barrier spell wouldn't last much longer.

"If we keep this up, we'll kill him!" shouted Jacob.

"I can take it from here," commanded the Queen.

Jacob quickly broke off the lightning spell with Elliot and Johnathan followed suit as they fell to their knees exhausted. The flames of the Queen's fire spell now swirled around Thomas with such an intense heat that Jacob had to shield his face with his robe's sleeve. He looked over at Captain Florentina who had successfully defeated what was left of the Farland guard. The Lady Regent Catherine was now running over to tend to her son Kiron and Neville.

Even though Queen Ellaryne was almost passing out from the magic she was performing, she still emitted the fire from her hands at Thomas's barrier spell which was almost fully broken. Bright red cracks appeared within the barrier, growing longer and deeper until finally the barrier shattered and fell around Thomas. The Queen instantly dispelled the flames. The heat from the fire spell created deep groves in the ice around Thomas who was swaying and rocking from side to side, now on his knees in pure exhaustion. His eyelids heavy, he slowly lifted his head up to look at the Queen, his green eyes now dull and full of defeat. King Jean started walking slowly behind the Queen, Jacob, Elliot and Johnathan, his thin and wrinkled face contorted into a triumphant smile.

"This… can't… it cannot be. I am more powerful that any of you," said Thomas, the words barely making it out of his mouth.

"But not all of us, Thomas!" said the Queen as she looked back at Johnathan who was breathing heavily. "*Johnathan, bind him,*" continued the Queen.

Johnathan lifted himself back to his feet, placing one hand on Jacob's shoulder to balance himself. He walked over to Thomas, who stumbled to his feet and tried to swing his fist at Johnathan but it just caused him to lose balance again and fall to the floor as Johnathan dodged him. He quickly took Thomas's hands behind his back and moved his finger in a figure of eight motion over his wrists. A faint blue string of light appeared rope-like around Thomas's hands, binding his MagiPower tightly.

"*It's done. The binding spell is linked to the ley lines. He is no longer a threat to anyone,*" said Johnathan as he made his way back to the Queen's side, who nodded and placed one knee and a hand on the ground, steadying herself from the overwhelming tiredness that was now washing over her.

Jacob dragged his tired body closer to his mother. He pulled at her shoulder and hugged her tightly.

"*I'm so sorry… Our last conversation, I didn't understand before. I think I do now…*" Jacob said, his eyes filling with tears. She took his face in her hands and then looked at Elliot and Johnathan, smiling warmly.

"*I know... Jacob you've done so well... all of you. I'm so proud of you all. You've saved us and the Empire,*" said the Queen, with her own eyes starting to fill with tears. Thomas fell onto one side, barely conscious, blinking slowly as he stared down at the icy surface.

"*King Jean?*" The Queen looked behind her where King Jean was standing with his arms folded, staring down at the four of them with his wrinkly smile and faded brown eyes. "*Thank you for coming to our aid in a moment of desperate need,*" the Queen continued.

He nodded and then his smile left his face replaced by a deep frown as he looked over at Captain Florentina and lifted one finger and pointed at Jacob. Then, in a moment of pure confusion, the Captain and King Jean leaped forward, summoning pushing spells directed at the Queen, Jacob, Elliot and Johnathan, slamming them hard, face down on the icy surface, the freezing ice burning their cheeks as the spell pushed them harder and harder into the surface.

"*WHAT GOING ON?!*" shouted Elliot as he desperately tried to wriggle free in vain. Their fight with Thomas had exhausted them too greatly to summon any magic to fight back.

King Jean then stood over the Queen and performed the same binding spell that Johnathan had cast over Thomas. The Queens hands were now bound with her shouting in protest.

"*Just like I showed you, Captain,*" said King Jean as Captain Florentina cast the same binding spells on Jacob, Elliot and Johnathan.

King Jean now stepped backwards away from the Queen and motioned his hands in a circle, forcing the four of them to their knees and spinning them one hundred and eighty degrees to face him, their hands locked behind them.

"*Well, well, well… thank you for making this so easy for me!*" bellowed King Jean.

CHAPTER FOURTEEN

THE BETRAYAL

◆

"Jean? What is going on? I demand you release us at once!" said the Queen. King Jean laughed in reply and bent down to her eye level, staring straight into her eyes.

"You never saw this coming, did you?" King Jean said, leaning back up; he began to pace back and forth in front of the four of them.

"You see, all of this… even him!" King Jean pointed at Thomas who was still drifting in and out of consciousness.

"This has been planned since before you came to the throne all those years ago, Ella," King Jean continued.

"What are you talking about?" said the Queen with frustration in her voice.

The King laughed again in her face. *"When your father killed Thomas's parents, he came to me. He confided in me... he told me who they really were and that the boy escaped. He knew you would take his life for this crime and so... he asked me to find this boy and finish what he started. But, I knew then and there that this boy would one day return seeking vengeance and that with his lineage, he would be more powerful than any living person in this world, even you. So, I waited... and... I waited... until finally, a man with bright green eyes claiming to be the true blood descendent of King Colet, taking his rightful place as King of the Dark Knights, approached the Lady Regent here to open the barrier and allow the American Republic of Magic and their navy through to wage a war so that this King of the Dark Knights could take the British throne."* King Jean now motioned his hand towards Lady Regent Catherine who was still tending to Kiron's shoulder wound while Neville struggled to his feet, clutching his shoulder.

"But... the good Lady Regent here turned Thomas down," continued King Jean.

Jacob and his mother looked at each other, both of their eyes full of confusion.

King Jean clapped his hands together making them look back at him. *"That was until I convinced her otherwise. I told* her to ally with Thomas and that she and her White Islands would have my protection for doing so," King Jean said as he noticed Thomas was now moving back onto his knees behind the Queen.

"No! The White Islands are loyal to me! Catherine, you pledged to me!" barked Thomas, glaring at the Lady Regent.

"Oh, you silly boy! You are nothing more than a blunt instrument for my master plan! I needed you to wage war on the British Empire, to weaken them, to divide their people and kill their leadership and in the process, thin out your own numbers and those of your allies, namely the Americans, who posed a threat to me after the Empire was defeated! It was going so well until you only managed half the job, Thomas! The Queen survived along with her entire Royal Council and heir. To be honest, I thought I was going to have to cut my losses but then… wondering around my Finders Maze was the lovely Royal Lady Kerr and her dirty little friend the Passing Dome Caretaker sent to me by you, Ella! The Caretaker, who was so quick to tell me she had a son left in charge of the Dome while she was away, provided me with a perfect opportunity to continue my plan. It didn't take long for me to send word to her son Lennard that unless he told me King Jacob's every move, I would hurt his mother in ways he didn't know were possible. It's amazing what one will do for their mother… isn't that right, Jacob?" King Jean said as he looked down at Jacob with a half-smile.

"That is how Thomas knew you were coming back to Farland Island to rescue your father, Jacob. And how he knew your husband was going to retrieve the Parliamentary Members *from Dover Cliff... Oh sorry, didn't you know, Ella? Your son got married while you were sleeping!"* said King Jean looking back over his shoulder at the Queen. She looked at Jacob and Elliot, a single tear falling from her face.

"Yes, yes, yes. Of course, I had a MagiWolf master embedded from the start that was loyal to me and close enough to King Thomas to be able to pass this information on, without throwing any suspicion my way and well... the rest is history really. King Jacob, you told me your plan to defeat King Thomas and your father provided me with the means to imprison your MagiPower with ley line linked binding spells. No, I am not going to kill any of you. MagiFolk are divided and the last thing we need to do is make you all martyrs to the cause," King Jean continued.

"NOOOOOOO!" shouted Thomas with the last of his energy before falling backwards unconscious. The Queen looked back at him and then up at King Jean, her frown deep and eyes full of anger and rage.

"Why do any of this, Jean? We were friends," cried the Queen.

"I was your substitute for a father, Ella! Thomas was correct, you're weak and unfit to rule, all of you. You ask why I'm doing this? Thomas was also correct that the human world grows ever bigger while our numbers decline. I have lived a very long time, Ella, and you're not the only Queen I know. You see, the human world is poisoned and in the last hundred years alone, they have had more wars, disease and destruction than in the history of both our worlds combined. In short, their system is broken.

So... I struck a bargain with all the European Kings and Queens of the human world. Allow MagiFolk to live openly within their countries and reclaim our rightful lands within Europe and we would help them retake their place as the heads of state of their countries by annihilating their corrupt governments. The Queen of England and King of France were all too obliging in the agreement and the rest followed. You see, we maybe dwindling in number but one sorcerer is still worth a hundred of them and their weapons. Oh, and of course, I will be made King of all MagiFolk, uniting all the Kingdoms and your fallen Empire... It's beautiful, isn't it!?" King Jean said triumphantly.

"*You're insane!*" said the Queen hanging her head low. "*You cannot trust the humans. They will never allow us to live openly. Mark my words, Jean, as soon as they have what they need from you, they will exterminate us,*" continued the Queen.

"*Tell me, Ella, how many humans have you met in your life?*" asked King Jean. The Queen shook her head slowly. "*Yes, that's what I thought. Captain? Take them away!*" commanded King Jean.

Captain Florentina walked over with her soldiers, motioning them around the Queen, Elliot, Jacob, Johnathan and Thomas.

"*Where do you want them, sire?*" asked Florentina. The King walked to the edge of the icy, cracked surface and looked back over his shoulder at the Captain.

"*The dungeons on Farland should do nicely. Don't worry... you'll be kept together. After all, misery needs company. I'll have the guards keep you updated on your Empire, Ella. But I am afraid most of your Royal Council will have to be retired, especially that snobby Camilla Kerr. Oh, and when I say retired, you know I mean killed, yes? I don't want there to be any more confusion between us,*" replied King Jean, chuckling to himself sarcastically. He lifted himself in the air with an air spell and flew back down to his ship.

"*Mother? What are we going to do?*" Jacob asked desperately.

"*Survive,*" replied the Queen as she looked directly into Jacob's eyes. Somehow the faith and confidence shone through her eyes into Jacob's as they were all pulled to their feet by Captain Florentina and the French soldiers who formed a circle around them and Thomas, summoning air spells lifting them all into the sky above and towards the ruins of the Regent's Hall and the dungeons below.

CHAPTER FIFTEEN

LONDON FALLS

❖

A lone bright polished bronze warship sailed silently in the middle of the afternoon up the famous River Thames into the heart of the human capital city of London. The masking spells surrounding the warship kept it hidden from human eyes. All onboard were deathly silent as the crewmen manned the loaded cannons on the starboard side waiting for the captain to give his signal to fire.

As the warship approached the Houses of Parliament, it slowed to a stop. Inside the building, the Prime Minister's questions were in full swing with shouting from either side of the bench taking its normal course. All the ministers were completely unaware of the immense destruction and death that was coming in the moments to follow.

The Captain of the warship, a heavy-set man with a long grey beard and deep scar across his face that blinded one of his eyes, dressed in an all-white naval uniform, walked to the starboard side of his ship, looking out at the Houses of Parliament rising up in all their historic architectural glory. He then turned and looked down at his crewmen manning the cannons, placing both his hands on the polished bronze banister.

"By order of Emperor Jean of the United Empires of Magic, we strike a blow to the heart of human tyranny and their governments. The human Kings and Queens will finally stand by our side as we come out from the shadows and their governments fall!" announced the Captain, which was followed by a grand cheer from the French crew.

"*FIRE!*" ordered the Captain.

As soon as the order was given, more than twenty cannons were fired from the warship straight into the heart of the Houses of Parliament. The cannon balls were enriched with fire spells, causing them to implode, sucking in all that surrounded them before exploding in flames sending out thousands of shards of debris into the Thames. The cannon balls broke through the stone walls and into the House of Commons, exploding in fire, stone shards and glass, killing all inside instantly. The relentless attack caused the entire building to collapse in on itself. The humans walking the streets below began to run in fear and panic as the smoke and debris spread out across all of Westminster. As the Houses Parliament fell, the Captain gave a new order to target the huge clock tower of Big Ben. The crewmen readjusted their aim and fired the cannons again. The balls of fire flew through the air leaving a trail of dark smoke in their wake before striking the clock and base of the tower. Within seconds, Big Ben was falling into Westminster Bridge. The people below tried to run but most failed to escape the crashing weight of stone upon them. Helicopters and Royal Air Force jets flew overhead searching in vain to find where the attack was coming from.

"We have done what is needed for now. About course, take us back to the Imperial City," commanded the Captain.

Meanwhile, back on Farland Island, Emperor Jean was making his way down the dark and wet stone stairwell leading to the dungeons flanked by two of his personal guards.

The condensation from his breath gathered in the freezing and damp air as he exhaled. He walked the length of the long cavern with the cells on his right, faintly lit by the fire spheres glowing above the prisoner guards. He stopped at the last cell and looked inside and then summoned his own fire spell. Queen Ellaryne sat perfectly still, her legs crossed over each other. She stared right into the eyes of the Emperor who smiled at her as he reached into his thickly fur-lined robe pocket pulling out a piece of MagiChartam.

"It's been quite a few weeks, Your Majesty. I thought I'd bring you this update myself," said the Emperor.

"There is nothing I wish to hear from your lips, you traitor," snarled the Queen.

"Well, perhaps, but I am going to tell you anyway. There's good news and bad news... Let's start with the good news. The war is underway with the human world and the Queen of England couldn't be happier with our progress and the sight of her government being annihilated. She is their new head of state and her subjects have accepted her rule. Other such similar events have been happening throughout Europe! And now for the bad news... it seems your Royal Lady Kerr has escaped along with several members of the Royal Council and oddly enough, the Lady Regent's daughter and grandson," said the Emperor. The Queen subtly smiled, which Emperor Jean noticed.

"Ah yes, I thought you'd like that bit of news. You're going to tell me where they would go and why this Kendra and her baby are important enough for Lady Kerr to take them with her," said the Emperor.

"I don't know the answer to either of those questions... and even if I did, I wouldn't tell you," replied the Queen. The Emperor smiled and laughed loudly, echoing through the cavern.

"We will see how you feel about that after your son is taken for some... rehabilitation, let's call it," snarled the Emperor. The Queen looked down at the wet, cold, black stone ground she was sitting upon and closed her eyes as three tears fell from her face.

"Hmmm. A parent's love for their child. Such a weakness. It's why I never had children," Emperor Jean said as he walked over to Jacob's cell. The Emperor's fire light flickered over

Jacob who was asleep on the stone floor, his robes torn and face bloodied.

"Oh, what fun I will have with you, young Prince. I wonder what secrets you have to tell," Emperor Jean chuckled evilly. *"Guards! Bring him up to the Regent's Hall at once!"* continued the Emperor as he turned on his heel back up the stone stairs, his dark fur robes trailing behind him.

"Welcome to the new world!" he shouted as he disappeared.

TO BE CONTINUED…

Thank you reading. Please leave a review of my book on Amazon.

ACKNOWLEDGEMENTS

I am indebted to my readers and friends for their support since I released my first book. Thank you to my family for their outstanding support and encouragement.

Printed in Great Britain
by Amazon